EXPLRER
ACADEMY

THE *TIGER'S NEST*

TRUDI TRUEIT

UNDER THE *Stars*

NATIONAL
GEOGRAPHIC

FOR AUSTIN, TRINA, BAILEY, AND CARTER, WHO MAKE ME THE LUCKIEST AUNT EVER —TT

Since 1888, the National Geographic Society has funded more than 12,000 research, exploration, and preservation projects around the world. The Society receives funds from National Geographic Partners, LLC, funded in part by your purchase. A portion of the proceeds from this book supports this vital work. To learn more, visit natgeo.com/info.

For more information, visit nationalgeographic.com, call 1-877-873-6846, or write to the following address:

National Geographic Partners
1145 17th Street N.W.
Washington, D.C. 20036-4688 U.S.A.

For librarians and teachers: nationalgeographic.com/books/librarians-and-educators

More for kids from National Geographic: natgeokids.com

National Geographic Kids magazine inspires children to explore their world with fun yet educational articles on animals, science, nature, and more. Using fresh storytelling and amazing photography, *Nat Geo Kids* shows kids ages 6 to 14 the fascinating truth about the world—and why they should care. **kids.nationalgeographic.com/subscribe**

For rights or permissions inquiries, please contact National Geographic Books Subsidiary Rights: bookrights@natgeo.com

Designed by Eva Absher-Schantz
Codes and puzzles developed by Dr. Gareth Moore

Hardcover ISBN: 978-1-4263-3862-5
Reinforced library binding ISBN: 978-1-4263-3863-2

Printed in Hong Kong
20/PPHK/1

PRAISE FOR THE EXPLORER ACADEMY SERIES

"A fun, exciting, and action-packed ride that kids will love."

—**J.J. Abrams,** award-winning film and
television creator, writer, producer, and director

"Inspires the next generation of curious kids to go out into our world and discover something unexpected."

—**James Cameron,** National Geographic
Explorer-in-Residence and acclaimed filmmaker

"...a fully packed high-tech adventure that offers both cool, educational facts about the planet and a diverse cast of fun characters."

—*Kirkus Reviews*

"Thrill-seeking readers are going to love Cruz and his friends and want to follow them on every step of their high-tech, action-packed adventure."

—**Lauren Tarshis,** author of the I Survived series

"Absolutely brilliant! Explorer Academy is a fabulous feast for mind and heart—a thrilling, inspiring journey with compelling characters, wondrous places, and the highest possible stakes. Just as there's only one planet Earth, there's only one series like this. Don't wait another instant to enjoy this phenomenal adventure!"

—**T.A. Barron,** author of the Merlin Saga

"Nonstop action and a mix of full-color photographs and drawings throughout make this appealing to aspiring explorers and reluctant readers alike, and the cliffhanger ending ensures they'll be coming back for more."

—*School Library Journal*

"Explorer Academy is sure to awaken readers' inner adventurer and curiosity about the world around them. But you don't have to take my word for it—check out Cruz, Emmett, Sailor, and Lani's adventures for yourself!"

—**LeVar Burton,** actor, director, author, and host
of the PBS children's series *Reading Rainbow*

"Sure to appeal to kids who love code cracking and mysteries with cutting-edge technology."

—*Booklist*

"I promise: Once you enter Explorer Academy, you'll never want to leave."

—**Valerie Tripp,** co-creator and author
of the American Girl series

"...the book's real strength rests in its adventure, as its heroes...tackle puzzles and simulated missions as part of the educational process. Maps, letters, and puzzles bring the exploration to life, and back matter explores the 'Truth Behind the Fiction'...This exciting series...introduces young readers to the joys of science and nature."

—*Publishers Weekly*

"Both my 8-year-old girl and 12-year-old boy LOVED this book. It's fun and adventure and mystery all rolled into one."

—**Mom blogger,** Beckham Project

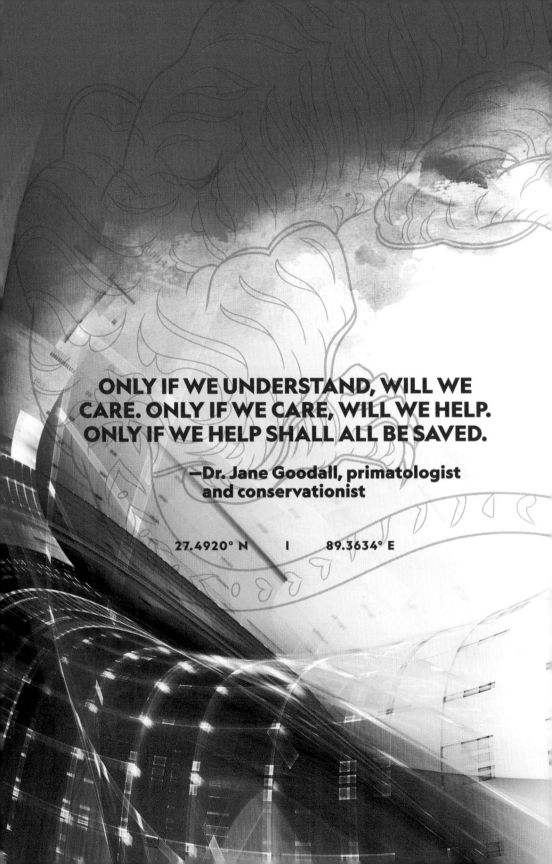

ONLY IF WE UNDERSTAND, WILL WE
CARE. ONLY IF WE CARE, WILL WE HELP.
ONLY IF WE HELP SHALL ALL BE SAVED.

—Dr. Jane Goodall, primatologist
and conservationist

27.4920° N   I   89.3634° E

SOMALIA
KENYA
TANZANIA
SEYCHELLES
ALDABRA
ATOLL,
SEYCHELLES
COMOROS
INDIAN
OCEAN
MOZAMBIQUE
MADAGASCAR

▶WHERE WAS ORION?

Seated beside Captain Roxas in the helicopter, Cruz scanned the blue swells below for a crest of white. Two days ago, Explorer Academy's flagship had sailed from Kenya. Without him.

First, a snowstorm had delayed Cruz's flight from New York, then mechanical problems with the plane had kept him grounded in Istanbul. Finally, he'd made it to Mombasa, where *Orion*'s helicopter pilot was waiting to fly him out to the ship in the western Indian Ocean.

Cruz had enjoyed semester break with his dad in Kauai. They'd worked at the Goofy Foot surf shop, ate their fill of pepperoni and sausage pizza with extra cheese, and surfed whenever they'd had a spare minute. It was like old times. Still, Cruz couldn't stop thinking about his mother's cell-regeneration formula. Four months ago, Cruz wasn't sure he'd be able to find even a single piece of the cipher and now he was halfway to his goal. Only four pieces to go! He was anxious to rejoin his friends and open the holo-journal for the fifth clue.

An angular silhouette appeared on the horizon. Cruz squinted against the glare of the noon sun off the ocean, his heart thumping so loudly he was sure Captain Roxas could hear it above the engine. Was that...?

It was! They'd found *Orion*. The ship, however, wasn't in motion. It had stopped a few miles west of an island.

Captain Roxas nodded to the elongated triangle of land. "Aldabra atoll."

The explorers had learned about Aldabra in Professor Ishikawa's class. The atoll was made up of a series of small islets that formed a reef around a lagoon. Part of the Seychelles outer islands, Aldabra was among Earth's largest coral reefs. No wonder the ship had dropped anchor here. It was an explorer's paradise! Approaching *Orion*, Cruz could see the Explorer Academy flag. It flew high above the bridge, a rippling beacon to welcome him home.

"Request: helicopter *Academy One* to *Orion*, permission to land," said Captain Roxas.

"Request granted," crackled the answer. "*Orion* standing by."

As they hovered above the helipad, Cruz tried to see into the oval roost on the ship's weather deck. He wondered if anyone had come up to meet him. Maybe his best friend? Lani had not traveled with Cruz to visit her own family in Kauai over the break. A new recruit with only a few weeks at the Academy under her belt, she had decided to stay behind to catch up on schoolwork and complete her required survival

training with Monsieur Legrand. Captain Roxas set the skids square in the middle of the giant *EA* on the pad so gently Cruz barely felt it. The pilot cut the engine and the blades spun to a stop.

Cruz flipped off his headset, unbuckled his seat belt, and hopped out of the aircraft the second the captain opened his door. "Thanks for the ride."

"Anytime." The pilot handed Cruz his duffel bag.

Cruz had barely set foot inside the roost when a fluffy white blob came hurtling toward him. He went to his knees and opened his arms.

"Woof!" Hubbard's pink tongue practically licked off his earlobe.

Laughing, Cruz fell over on the fall leaves rug.

"He's missed you." Taryn Secliff was standing behind one of the olive green chairs.

"I've missed him, too." It may have only been two and half weeks, but to Cruz, it felt like ages. Cruz rolled to his knees. He glanced around the empty room. It was a bit weird that *none* of his friends had come up to meet him. He hoped nothing was wrong.

"Don't worry." His adviser saw his frown. "You won't be in trouble for missing the mission."

"Mission?" Cruz gulped. "Already?" That would explain why nobody was here.

"The teams are exploring the reef around Aldabra in *Ridley*. Team Earhart went this morning. Cousteau is next." She glanced at her watch. "If you hurry, you might make it."

Holding Hubbard, Cruz scrambled to his feet. He planted a quick kiss on the dog's head before handing him off to Taryn. He sprinted for the door, then spun back. "My gear—"

"I'll take care of it." Taryn waved her free arm. "Go!"

"Woof!" barked Hubbard.

Cruz didn't need to be told again. Aquatics was on the lowest level of the ship—six decks down. He flew down flight after flight, the soles of his shoes squealing at every corner. He smacked his comm pin. "Cruz to Marisol Coronado."

"You're here!" came the enthusiastic reply. "I was just coming up to meet you. Hungry?"

"Kind...of."

"You want to swing by and we can—"

"Wish I could...can't."

"You sound out of breath. Are you running?"

"Team mission...*Ridley*. Do me...favor? Call Dad. Tell him...I'm back."

"Sure. Have fun."

"Thanks, *Tía*. Cruz, out." He flew off the bottom step of the last flight of steps onto B deck. Swinging around a post, Cruz catapulted himself into the maze of corridors that led to aquatics. His lungs were heaving by the time he reached the outer door of the submarine bay. Planting his palms on each side of the round window, Cruz peered through the glass. *Nooooo!*

The compartment was filled with seawater. Through the greenish blue haze he could make out the tip of *Ridley*'s tail moving through the opening in the ship's hull. He was late. Again. Panting, Cruz could do nothing but watch the bay door close behind the sub.

"Missed your ride, huh?" Fanchon Quills was coming up behind him. The science tech lab chief was carrying fins and a diving helmet. Her caramel curls, the tips dyed sunset orange, spilled out of a black-and-pink-striped head scarf. Wearing an MC camera headset, the lens flipped up, Fanchon looked like a butterfly with one antenna.

"My team went to check out the reef in *Ridley*. Without me."

"So?"

Cruz gave her a puzzled look. What was he supposed to do? Swim after them?

"Give 'em a shout," she urged.

"You think they'd come back?"

Fanchon smirked. "I'm no pilot but I'm pretty sure the sub can turn."

Cruz hit his comm pin. "Cruz Coronado to ... uh ..."

He had no idea who to ask for. *Orion* didn't have a sub pilot, not since Tripp Scarlatos.

"Jaz," prompted Fanchon.

"Huh?"

"Dr. Jazayeri is the new aquatics director. Came in over break. Goes by Jaz."

He got it. "Cruz Coronado to Jaz."

"Jaz here," replied a woman.

"I'm on Team Cousteau. I got back a few minutes ago ... I saw you leave ... I know it's probably too late but ..." He gave Fanchon a helpless look.

There was a long silence.

"We're coming about now, Cruz," said Jaz. "Meet us at the aft deck of aquatics."

Cruz rocketed into the air. "I'll be right there! Cruz, out."

"Hold on," said the tech lab chief when Cruz would have taken off. Fanchon removed her MC camera and placed it on Cruz's head. "You'll need this."

"Thanks, Fanchon!" Cruz hurried down the corridor. A minute later, he was on the port stern watching the giant bubble that was *Ridley* rise up out of the waves. Jaz expertly maneuvered the vehicle to within a few feet of *Orion*'s back deck, making it easy for Cruz to jump to the sub's ladder. Scampering up the rungs, he dropped through the top hatch she'd opened for him. Emmett, Lani, Bryndis, Sailor, and Dugan were seated in a semicircle around a woman in the pilot's seat. Jaz had olive skin and wide dark gray eyes rimmed in purplish black eyeliner. She'd twisted her long black hair into a side ponytail, and a gold hoop earring was caught in her thick hair. "Welcome aboard!"

"Thanks for doing a U-turn."

"No problem."

Cruz moved past Bryndis to sit at the end of the bench. Her fair hair was braided into two loose pigtails. Pale blue eyes glanced up at Cruz. She smiled. He melted. And stumbled. Emmett caught him before he did a face-plant. Sailor put a hand to her mouth, but it did little to mute her snort.

Jaz nodded to the empty seat next to her. "You can sit here if you want."

"That's perfect!" exclaimed Lani. "Jaz, Cruz is a sub pilot, too.

"Not officially," corrected Cruz. He slid into the copilot's seat. "I went through all the training, though I ... uh ... never actually took *Ridley* out of *Orion*'s docking bay. But hey, I'm a great pilot on land."

That got a laugh.

A joystick in each hand, Jaz backed the sub away from the *Orion*. Once they were about 20 feet from the ship, Jaz tapped her computer screen and they heard a whirring noise. The ballast tanks on each side of the vehicle began venting. Cruz knew the tanks were used for buoyancy. They released air, allowing the sub to sink. To rise, the pilot filled the tanks with air from the compressor. The submarine slowly descended beneath the choppy waves.

"*Ridley* to *Orion*. We are good to dive, dive, dive," Jaz said into her headset.

The sub glided through the turquoise waters at a downward angle. Jaz flipped on the headlights. Hundreds of silvery blue fish parted, half darting left and the other half zipping right. Cruz wondered how they decided who went which way.

"Some people think we've explored every inch of the Earth and there's nothing left to see," said Jaz. "If only they could come down here. We figure that at least one-third of life under the sea is still undiscovered. Since there may be as many as a million different species in the oceans, that leaves plenty for you guys and your kids and their kids to find!" She'd no sooner spoken the words than a spotted eagle ray glided toward them. Its triangular fins flapped like wings in the water.

"It's so beautiful," cooed Sailor.

"It's so big," gasped Emmett.

"It's so . . . leaving," said Jaz, as the ray's long, thin tail tapped her side of the bubble. "Start taking photos, explorers. Your MC cameras are connected to *Orion*'s computer, so you'll also get identification data on your subjects—unless, of course, you discover a new species."

Everyone began snapping pictures. Cruz aimed his camera at a spinning vortex of yellow Bengal snappers, thought of the word "photo," and shut his eyes for the required two seconds. When he opened them, he saw a tubular trumpetfish swimming vertically. Cruz took another picture. After that came a spotted potato grouper; an orange, black, and white-striped Seychelles anemonefish; and a silvery white geometric moray eel with black dots sprinkled on its head. The little spots in a geometric pattern practically dared you to connect them. Cruz couldn't capture all the action fast enough.

Soon, a rocky bulge emerged from the blue haze. "We're coming up on the atoll's barrier reef," said Jaz. She was giving Cruz a sideways glance. "Wanna drive?"

"You mean it?"

"I do." She handed him his own headset, grabbed her tablet, and they swapped seats.

Removing his MC camera, Cruz replaced it with the radio headset and settled in behind the console. Cruz wrapped his hands around the

right and left joysticks. At last! It was happening. He was piloting *Ridley*!

Jaz bent toward him. "I confess, I read the former AD's log. He mentioned you."

Cruz swallowed hard. "H-he did?"

"He said you were an excellent student and ready to pilot *Ridley* under supervision."

It was a comfort to know that Tripp thought Cruz was up to the task—a small comfort, considering the former sub pilot had also tried to kill him.

"*Ridley*, *Ridley*, Topside." Cruz heard a man's voice over his headset. He swung to Jaz, who nodded for him to answer *Orion*'s call.

"Topside, *Ridley*," said Cruz. "Go ahead."

"Yeah, *Ridley*, time for a comm check."

"Copy that, Topside," said Cruz. "We are currently holding at eighty-nine feet."

"Ready for readings," said the *Orion* crewman.

Jaz was pointing to the oxygen gauges, to remind him, but Cruz knew what to do.

"Main oxygen, twenty-one hundred PSI," reported Cruz. "Reserve oxygen, twenty-eight hundred PSI."

"Main twenty-one, reserve twenty-eight," echoed the crewman.

"Cabin pressure is half a PSI above one ATM," said Cruz. "Life support systems are good. Visibility is about fifty feet. Continuing our descent."

"Copy that, *Ridley*. Have a good dive."

Jaz gave him an approving grin. It had been a test. And Cruz had passed.

Scanning the teal waters, Cruz sat taller. He eased the left joystick forward. The sub responded, gently banking to the right. Driving a sub really wasn't much different than playing a video game. The controls were virtually identical. As they neared the seafloor, Cruz leveled out the sub. This was fun—and not nearly as hard as he'd expected!

Uh-oh.

Cruz stiffened. He'd been following the edge of the reef, but now some kind of bulge or wall stretched out in front of them. It was directly in their path. He saw a hole in the rocky barrier, but it looked awfully small. It didn't help that large clusters of staghorn coral guarded each side of the gap. Should he bank left and look for a way around? Or keep going. "Uh . . . Jaz?"

"I see it," she said. "It's wide enough. Give it a tad more on the starboard thruster to line us up."

Cruz's shirt was sticking to his back. He was holding the controls so tightly his hands were going numb. Approaching the opening in the reef, Cruz slowed the sub. *Ridley* slipped between the spikes of antler-like coral. Cruz held his breath. By the silence behind him, he had a feeling everyone else was doing the same.

Please don't scrape, please don't scrape, he prayed.

Not hearing a sound, Cruz glanced back. They had cleared the coral! His teammates were smiling. Dugan gave him a thumbs-up.

"Well done," proclaimed Jaz. "I know this is your first dive, but it will help if you can relax your death grip on those joysticks a little."

"Right." Cruz flexed his fingers. He continued on, getting close enough to the reef ledge on the starboard side to give his team more photo ops, yet also making sure to maintain a safe distance. Lani got some great shots of a brain coral. The six-foot brownish bulb with its twisting grooves really did look like a human brain.

Cruz was checking his gauges again when a torpedo streaked across *Ridley*'s bow!

"Whoa!" cried Dugan. "What was *that*?"

"A blacktip reef shark," Jaz said calmly.

A five-foot gray shark, its fins and tail looking as if they had been dipped in black paint, was circling them. A pointed snout turned

slightly and Cruz saw its mouth, gills, and light gray underbelly. Cruz
had seen sharks at home, of course, but from a distance and from the
surface. The blacktip was powerful, yet graceful, as it sailed through
the water. Cruz didn't want to hit or scare the animal, so he slowed the
sub and kept his course straight and true.

"Nice," Jaz said quietly. "Exactly how I would have done it."

The shark went past the windshield once more before swimming
away. Jaz signaled it was time to head back to *Orion*. Cruz made a wide
turn over a bed of seagrass, attracting the attention of a green turtle.
The reptile swam up to Cruz's window. It was huge! Its mottled brown
carapace had to be close to the width of a monster truck tire—maybe
bigger. Cruz knew that the green turtle was named for its pale green
skin. The turtle leveled off, its flippers easily stroking to match *Ridley*'s
speed. A head turned and a hooded eyeball peered at them.

"He's probably trying to figure out what kind of creature we are,"
said Emmett.

Sailor snickered. "We need Fanchon to make us a Universal Reptile
Communicator."

"If anyone could do it, she could," said Cruz.

The inquisitive reptile stayed with them for several hundred yards before veering off. As they neared *Orion*, Cruz flipped on the air compressor to fill the ballast tanks. The sub began to ascend. His sonar showed they were within a few hundred yards of *Orion*. Jaz should be taking over the controls. Unless...

Cruz swallowed hard. She wasn't planning on letting him dock the sub, was she? Jaz was making no effort to move. Jaz?" Cruz stared at her. "You should probably take us in..."

"You can do it." Her tone was gentle but firm. "You've practiced it in your head, haven't you?"

"A million times, but this is *real*. This is—"

"Every pilot has a first docking. Don't overthink it. One step at a time." She rested her hand against the copilot's console. "And I'm not going anywhere."

"O-okay."

One step at time, huh? Okay. Deep breath.

What did he need to do first? Contact the ship. Cruz clicked on his headset. "Topside, this is ... uh ... *Ridley*." Geez! Cruz had nearly forgotten the name of the sub! "We're ... uh ... seventy-nine feet from the ship on a south-southeast heading at a depth of twenty-five feet. Request: Open the sub bay door."

"Topside," came the reply. "Request received. Opening sub bay door."

Out of the haze in front of them, the ship's hull appeared. Cruz could see the opening in the stern. He leveled off and lined up with the bay. They were about thirty feet from the ship when Jaz said, "We're close enough now to let momentum take us in."

Cruz eased up on the throttle, reminding himself to relax his grip. He held his breath, as if, somehow, he could get *Ridley* into the bay by sheer will. They were almost there ...

"Steady as she goes," whispered Jaz.

Silently and smoothly, *Ridley* slipped into *Orion*'s belly.

Cruz wanted to celebrate, but his job wasn't done yet. Once they'd cleared the door, Cruz extended the catch arms, which grabbed the ropes attached to the bay walls. With a couple of gentle bounces, the sub came to a full stop. Cruz released the anchor and shut off the motor. "*Orion,* docking is complete."

"Thank you, *Ridley.* Welcome back."

Cruz let out the biggest, happiest breath of his life. He'd done it— his first sub dive!

They waited while a deckhand drained water from the compartment. Jaz popped *Ridley*'s hatch and Team Cousteau climbed out, one after the other. Cruz stayed to assist the aquatics director as she checked the tanks, batteries, and equipment. He was the last explorer out.

Cruz scampered down the ladder to join his team, who'd waited for him. "Hey, was that cool or—"

Suddenly, a tidal wave washed over him! The shock of cold water made Cruz jump. His uniform was totally drenched. Cruz threw out his arms. "What the...?"

Sailor, Emmett, Lani, Bryndis, and Dugan were laughing. Dugan was holding a bucket.

"Congrats on your first submarine dive!" Emmett led the team in a round of applause. "You earned your lemonade bath."

Cruz brought his fingers to his lips and felt a sweetly sour sting. It *was* lemonade. He glanced up to where Jaz had appeared at *Ridley*'s top hatch. By her satisfied grin, he knew she'd had something to do with setting up the ritual. Like a wet dog, Cruz shook the juice from his hair. He pretended to be annoyed with his friends. But he wasn't. Not really. He was proud.

Sticky. But proud.

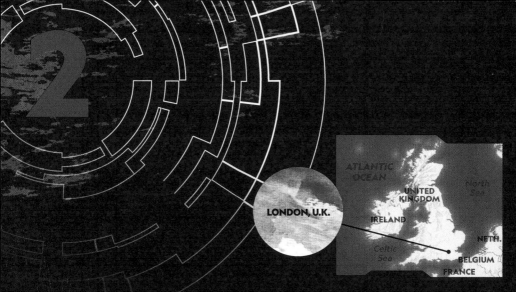

ATLANTIC
OCEAN

UNITED
KINGDOM

North
Sea

LONDON, U.K.

IRELAND

NETH.

Celtic
Sea

BELGIUM

FRANCE

▶**THORNE PRESCOTT** *peered between lacy palms and tree ferns. This was ridiculous. He felt like a clumsy spy in a bad movie.*

Sliding his sunglasses onto his head, his gaze traveled up to the metal walkway that ran the perimeter of the grand Victorian-era greenhouse. Scanning the white metal catwalk, Prescott saw school-age kids, teachers, and parents. He did not, however, see the man he'd come for.

Prescott had agreed to meet Malcolm Rook in the Temperate House of the Kew Botanical Gardens in London. He knew what the former Explorer Academy librarian and ousted Nebula Pharmaceuticals agent was up to. Rook planned to get the cipher from Cruz Coronado, then sell it to the highest bidder, which in all likelihood would be Hezekiah Brume, the head of Nebula. What Prescott didn't know was how Rook was going to do it. And why. Rook must have known that if Brume so much as caught a whiff of where his former spy was, his life wouldn't be worth a cent. Was he doing it for the challenge? Revenge? Money? All three?

Prescott wasn't convinced that teaming with Rook was a good idea. First, Rook may no longer have been working for Brume, but Prescott still was. He had everything to lose, while Rook had everything to gain. Second, Prescott wasn't sure he could trust Rook. Strike that. He knew he couldn't trust Rook.

Several teenagers were coming his way. Prescott bent, pretending to be interested in a plant with heart-shaped leaves and dainty bell blossoms the color of butter. He read the sign:

Yellow Fatu *(Abutilon pitcairnense)*
Native to Pitcairn Island, yellow fatu was once thought to be extinct. In the early 20th century, a single plant was discovered on the island. Cuttings and seeds were collected, and the species was grown in the island's nursery. Soon after, a landslide destroyed the last surviving plant. Due to habitat loss, yellow fatu is now extinct in the wild.

The group passed and turned at the next intersecting pathway. What had Rook been thinking? This place was too public. Too big. The 200-year-old restored greenhouse was the length of a couple of football fields. It was a jungle. Prescott could be poking around plants all day and never find—
    "Morning."

Rook. Prescott gave a slight nod to the man with bushy red hair. The way the sun was shining through the glass roof, it painted prison-bar shadows on Rook's gray wool coat.

"Here we are among the rarest plants on Earth," said Rook. "A fitting place to discuss things, I thought, given the prize at stake."

Prescott had no patience for arrogance masking as intelligence. "You have five minutes." Clasping his hands behind his back, he continued down the path.

Rook fell in step beside him. "Lion—I mean, Brume—has two spies on board Orion."

Zebra and Jaguar. Prescott knew.

"And you want to turn one of them so he's loyal to you," said Prescott.

Rook gave an evil chuckle. "Already have."

"What do you want from me— Ah!" It hit him. "You need money."

"Only half. I'll put up the other half. Fifty-fifty partners."

Prescott doubted that. Rook didn't seem like the kind of guy who would split power equally. "I don't need a partner," said Prescott. "I already have a job."

"You won't need one after this. I've got it all worked out. Don't worry."

Prescott bristled. Usually, when someone said "don't worry" there was plenty to worry about.

"Cruz only has four pieces," said Rook. "He needs eight. I figure the spy gets us intel, and we get to one of them before he does."

Prescott's head whipped around. "You're saying we should go for the cipher ourselves?"

"Who better? We can't trust anyone else."

"What makes you think I trust you?"

"Hey, for all I know, you're here to handle me for Brume."

Prescott waited for a woman to pass. "You're safe from me."

"For now," shot Rook.

He was right. Prescott could tell Brume everything Rook was up to, then pick his time and place to deal with the former spy. That's what he got paid for, after all—to make Brume's problems disappear. And boy, was Malcolm Rook ever a problem.

Prescott paused to inspect a strange-looking palm plant. A bright orange cone at least two feet long rose from the center of a round trunk. The cone was surrounded by a crown of long, thin fern leaves.

Wood's Cycad (*Encephalartos woodii*)
Only one specimen of Wood's cycad has ever been found in the wild. It was discovered on the edge of South Africa's Ngoye Forest in 1895 by English botanist John Medley-Wood (for whom the plant is named). Kew's specimen arrived in 1899 but did not produce its first cone until 2004. All Wood's cycads are clones of the last wild specimen, so all are male. Until a female of the species is discovered, this plant remains without a mate.

Sad, *thought Prescott.*

Rook cleared his throat. He was waiting for an answer.

But Prescott's trained eye had spotted something, or rather someone, through the branches of the cycad tree. Tipping his head, he saw a flash of red. It looked like the swinging hem of a jacket. Someone was watching them!

Leaping over the sign, Prescott bolted straight into the display of rare plants. He fought his way through the thicket of trees and shrubs. He tried not to trample the exhibits, but it couldn't be helped. Pushing aside the long, slender leaves of a vine, Prescott felt his foot hit something hard. He was back on a path. Huffing, he glanced left. Nobody. He swung right. About 10 yards off, a teen girl was walking away from him. She was wearing a pink sweater and jeans, a small blue backpack with white polka dots slung over one shoulder. Straight ahead, about 20 yards away, was an open door.

Prescott took off, his boots clanging against the metal grate of the wide aisle. Once outside, he pulled up short at the top of the concrete steps. The lawn stretched out in all directions from the main walkway, a massive green carpet as far as the eye could see. People were sitting on benches and strolling down the pathways. Prescott saw red everywhere—in the lace of a shoe and the stripe of a bag and the rim of cap—but not on a coat. Either he was imagining things or . . .

Whoever was spying on them was gone.

"MANDATORY merriment!" Emmett knocked on Sailor and Bryndis's door, while Cruz hurried ahead to get Lani.

Dugan had come out of his cabin, too. He joined Emmett, Sailor, and Bryndis, who then caught up to Lani and Cruz. Now together, Team Cousteau was ready for Funday.

Lani led the way to the atrium. "I wonder what we're doing."

"As long as it's not cooking, I'm good." Cruz slapped Emmett on the back.

"Hey, I thought you liked my chocolate-covered, bacon-wrapped fried Swiss cheese squares," said his roommate.

"You thought wrong."

"I liked 'em," piped up Sailor. "The worst Funday was when Taryn had us make musical instruments. Talk about torture."

"Felipe's guitar sounded like a sick cow." Dugan let out a low-pitched wail.

"He's not exaggerating," Cruz said to Lani as they went up the grand staircase.

She laughed. "I guess that's one good thing about enrolling late."

"I heard a rumor we're crocheting bunny slippers," said Bryndis.

Cruz groaned. Seriously? He knew Taryn liked to crochet but he was hoping for something exciting, something challenging, something FUN!

After all, it was called *Fun*day.

Taryn had started the tradition soon after the explorers had come aboard *Orion*. Their adviser had noticed they were a bit, as she'd put it, stressed out. She'd proclaimed that every Sunday afternoon thereafter would be known as Funday. Each week, she devised a different activity for them to do. She said it was a way for the explorers to get better acquainted and try new things without the fear of being graded. Originally, Cruz wasn't sure about Taryn's mandatory merriment, as Emmett had put it, but now he looked forward to it. Unless, of course, Bryndis was right and they were making bunny slippers. He was not looking forward to that.

Cousteau was the last team to arrive in the third-deck conference room. Taryn stood at the far end of the room. Cruz looked around for her yarn bag but didn't see it. Good sign. Fanchon was there, too, setting up a 3D printer in one corner of the room. Another positive sign!

Five shiny red fingernails were tapping the big oval table. It was two o'clock. Their adviser did not like to be kept waiting. Twenty-four explorers quickly found their seats.

Taryn glanced around the room, her gaze going from explorer to explorer. "Today's Funday activity is . . ."

The room went silent.

Cruz held his breath, crossed his fingers, and hoped no yarn was involved.

Taryn's green eyes sparkled. "Robotics!"

The place erupted.

This was what they'd been waiting for. Cruz fist-bumped each of his teammates.

"I'm glad you approve." Their adviser's voice rose above the cheers. "We're going to work in six groups of four."

The celebrating abruptly stopped. Their mission teams were made up of six members each. Four groups of six meant Taryn planned to break up the teams! Cruz glanced nervously down the table. His gaze went from Bryndis to Emmett to Sailor to Lani, and came to rest on Dugan. Which two of them were going to get tossed out? A buzz went through the room. Some of the explorers started latching on to each other to signal they were a team. Kwento, across the table, was stretching toward Cruz. "Do you want to—"

"Explorers!" Taryn's voice sliced through the chatter. "I've already grouped you, so you can relax. You'll be matched with classmates you may not have had the chance to work with in the past. I know I'm throwing you a curve, but I'm confident you're up to the challenge."

Cruz's stomach tightened. What if he was in Ali's group? Ali was still mad at Cruz for leaving him behind when they'd rescued Bryndis in Uganda. Cruz held his breath until Taryn announced he was with Weatherly, Shristine, and Felipe.

"You may build any type of robot you like—as long as it isn't destructive or violent, of course," instructed Taryn. "Remember our school motto."

They knew it by heart: *To discover. To innovate. To protect.*

Cruz huddled with his team at one end of the long wooden table.

"I know this isn't supposed to be a competition," whispered Weatherly, "but let's come up with something cool to blow everyone's minds."

"I agree," said Felipe. "No boring boxes."

"How about a bot that flies?" suggested Shristine.

"I don't know." Felipe nudged Cruz. "We don't want to make Mell jealous."

They laughed.

"Taryn's always doing stuff for us," said Weatherly. "Let's make a bot to help her."

Felipe tipped his head. "You mean, like an assistant?"

"She's already got cleaning bots, like the rest of us," said Shristine. "And she uses her tablet for organizing everything else. What's left?"

"Hubbard," mumbled Cruz, an idea forming.

"What did you say, Cruz?" pressed Felipe.

"Hubbard," he repeated. "What if we made him a robot dog pal that he could play with on his own, you know, when Taryn's busy?"

Weatherly grinned. "Now *that* is what I'm talking about."

Felipe bobbed his head. "Let's take a vote. All in favor?"

Four hands went up.

Now the question was, what kind of pal could keep a dog busy?

"How about a disk?" suggested Felipe.

"Maybe a stick?" said Shristine.

"Hubbard likes balls the best," said Cruz.

Wrinkling her freckled nose, Weatherly tugged on the end of her braid. "Well, we can't do them all."

"Why not?" piped up a voice from behind him. Cruz turned to see Fanchon, tying on a black head scarf sprinkled with tiny yellow stars. "You could make a wireless companion that syncs up to Hubbard's brain waves and transforms into whatever he wants to play with that day— ball, stick, or disk."

Cruz's jaw fell. "We could do that?"

Fanchon hooked a thumb around the shoulder strap of a peacock blue apron that read *Eat. Sleep. Science. Repeat.* "Might take us a few tries to get it working correctly, and Hubbard is an uncertain variable. We can only hope he isn't the sort of dog that changes his mind often but, yeah, it's possible."

Weatherly laughed. "Fanchon, you think everything's possible."

Fanchon raised an eyebrow. "Isn't it?"

"But how do we design a bot pal with all three things?" asked Shristine.

"I'm sure such clever minds as yours can come up with an innovative solution," said the tech lab chief, using that tone adults use when they feel they have helped you enough. "I've got to circulate among the other teams, but I'll check back in a while." Before moving on, Fanchon bent next to Cruz. "I need to talk to you," she whispered. "Tech lab, tomorrow morning before breakfast?"

Cruz gave her a quick nod. He reached for his stylus to begin working. Everyone in his group did individual sketches first, then they combined the best features of each to create a design they all liked. The main part of the robot was a lightweight rubberlike ring. A partial section, about a third of the outer rim, separated to become a curved stick. The third part, a ball, fit snugly in the middle of the disk and could easily pop out. This way, Hubbard could play with one, two, or all three items!

Cruz studied their final drawing. He chewed his lip. "It reminds me of something."

"Saturn," chirped Shristine.

"That's what it is! It looks like the planet Saturn."

"That's what we should call it," said Felipe. "Planet Pup."

The perfect name for the perfect dog pal.

"Excellent," said Fanchon when they showed her their sketch. "I knew you could do it."

Taryn was impressed, too. "Hub is going to love this!"

The next step for the team was to plug their design into the software and make a 3D prototype on the printer. After that, they inserted the guts of the robot: servo motors, controller boards, and batteries. Finally, they had to program the bot and remote controller. It wasn't complicated, but they did encounter some problems. Some of the issues were big, like getting a disk with a detachable section to balance evenly so it could fly, while others were little, such as a loose wire on a controller that took Cruz forever to find. Almost four hours later, when Felipe announced "I think we're ready!" only Cruz, Shristine, Weatherly, and Fanchon remained in the conference room. All the other teams had long since gone to dinner. Even Taryn had left to feed Hubbard.

"We still need Fanchon's help to make a unit that syncs it with Hubbard's brain waves," said Felipe. "But we can put it through a few tests now with our basic remote." He presented Cruz with the robot. "After all, it was your idea."

They had programmed the disk to hover for five seconds and then smoothly sail above the ground for a length of 15 feet or so to give Hubbard time to run, jump, and catch it. Crouching, Cruz glanced back over his shoulder at his teammates and Fanchon. They had backed into the corner behind him to give him space. Shristine was holding the remote. If anything went wrong, she could quickly shut down Planet Pup.

Cruz tapped the flat power button on the top inside rim of the disk. He heard the low, even hum of a motor. Extending his arm, Cruz released the machine. It floated in front of him. So far, so good. His teammates let out a soft cheer. It appeared they had solved the balance issue. Cruz got down on all fours so he could chase it the way Hubbard would.

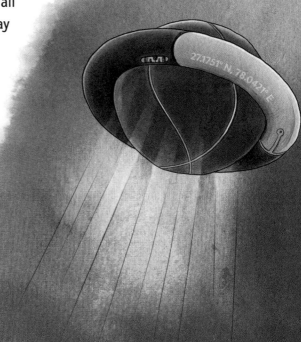

Suddenly, the disk lurched upward. Almost as quickly, it dropped down to within a few inches of the floor, then zipped up again. It wasn't supposed to do that! When it came down for the third time, Cruz reached for the power button but missed. The motor revved. The disk spun, then went backward, smacking Cruz on the forehead. It flew straight up, hit the ceiling, and spiraled down to bounce off the table. Shristine was punching the remote but the bot didn't stop. In fact, it was picking up speed as it ricocheted off the ceiling and walls.

"I can't control it!" cried Shristine.

"Everyone get down!" ordered Fanchon.

Cruz dropped to the floor, going flat on his stomach. He flung his arms over his head and locked his fingers behind his skull. All he could see was chair legs, but he could hear plenty. The disk was bouncing off things. Glass was shattering. Cruz tightened his grip. Then . . .

Silence.

The bot must have run out of power. That, or Shristine had finally gotten the remote to respond. Cruz went up on his knees. Everyone else was getting up, too. Cruz scanned the room but didn't see the disk. Oh no! It must have flown out of the room. It was probably hurtling down the passage. The atrium was several decks high. All that glass!

Cruz sprang to his feet and was about to charge out when he saw Taryn in the doorway. She had her coffee cup in one hand and Planet Pup in the other.

Cruz's chin dropped. "How did you—"

"I have my ways." Their adviser gave a wry grin. "Sure you don't want to call it Meteor Pup?"

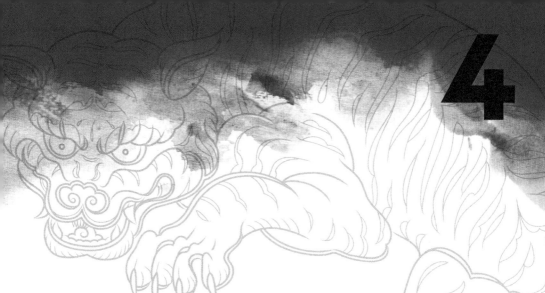

4

▶ **"CRIKEY!"** cried Sailor. "Your bot really went bonkers?"

Cruz's shoulders fell. "Yep."

"Too bad." Lani took a spot on the floor between the two overstuffed navy chairs in Cruz and Emmett's cabin. The explorers could hear Felipe practicing his violin next door. "It was a great idea."

"Was?" shot Cruz. "We're not giving up. Fanchon's going to help us iron out the kinks."

"While you're at it you'd better throw in a safety helmet for Hubbard," joked Emmett, not taking his eyes from his trio of desktop computers.

Lani's lips twitched. "Maybe include a box of bandages."

"Or a vet visit." Sailor fell into one of the big chairs.

"Funny," moaned Cruz, kneeling next to Lani.

"We're only teasing." She put a hand on his shoulder. "We'll stop."

"Besides, it's not like our groups did anything even close to that amazing," said Sailor. "We made our box robot dance, if spinning in a circle is considered dancing. The bloody thing kept losing a foot and we never could get it to go clockwise."

"My group made a mouse robot that could go through a maze. Kid stuff, really," said Lani. "Emmett, what did your team do?"

"Uh … one sec …" He was typing. "Still working on it. We … um … made extend."

Sailor scrunched her nose. "What's extend? Like, a bot that grows?"

"*EggsTend,*" enunciated Emmett. Turning, he hung an arm over the back of his chair and opened his palm to reveal what looked to be a small cream-colored egg. "It monitors sea turtle nests. I read an article about how scientists put GPS tracking devices inside fake turtle eggs to catch poachers *after* they steal eggs and I thought, what if we could make a robot egg that could actually protect the nest? You know, scare the poachers away *before* they steal the eggs." He took a big breath. "Here's how it works: Once a mother turtle lays her eggs, the EggsTend here locates the nest and digs its way down to the clutch. It keeps tabs on things all season long, sending data and photos back to the conservation center. It can identify the type of eggs, count them, and record the temperature. The bot is also a motion detector. If it senses motion from the top, it sends an alert to the conservation team that a poacher or animal has found the nest and a siren will sound to scare the invader away. If it picks up movement from beneath, which means the eggs are hatching, it tells the team that, too, so they can send volunteers to protect the hatchlings as the little guys scurry to the sea. When all the baby turtles in the nest have

hatched, the EggsTend surfaces and finds a new nest to monitor."

Dumbfounded, Cruz, Lani, and Sailor could only stare at him.

"What?" Emmett's emoto-glasses became sapphire crescent moons. "You don't like it?"

"Uhhh…" sputtered Sailor.

"We like it," said Cruz. "We just can't believe it."

Lani was shaking her head. "You did all that in one afternoon?"

"I've been thinking about it for a while. And we're not done yet." Emmett nodded to his computer. "I'm still coding. But I have a good team—Kwento, Kat, and Blessica. Fanchon is helping, too."

"Well done, *egg*-splorer," said Cruz.

"Thanks." Emmett placed the egg robot on the edge of his desk. "We think it's pretty *egg*-cellent."

Sailor rolled her eyes. "This is getting *egg*-scruciating!"

"Yeah," Lani chimed in, laughing. "Can you eggheads cut it out?"

Emmett came to take the chair opposite Sailor. "But it's so—"

"Don't you dare say *egg*-citing!" she snapped.

"I wasn't going to."

"Good."

"I was going to say *egg*-straordinary."

Sailor slammed a penguin pillow to her face. They heard a muffled scream.

Cruz couldn't resist. "Stand back," he shouted, "she's going to *egg*-splode!"

Lani and Emmett laughed.

"Emmett." Cruz's tone turned serious. "You do realize what you've done, don't you? Only about one in a thousand sea turtles survives to adulthood. The EggsTend could help save an entire species."

Emmett beamed. He knew.

With the evening ticking away, it was time to get down to business. Cruz slid his mom's holo-journal out of Lani's protective sleeve and placed it in the middle of the low, round table. He got to his feet. Flaps appeared from the flat white square. They unfolded like the petals of a flower. The blossoming was followed by self-origami, a rapid succession of folds and creases that transformed the journal into a multi-pointed sphere. The orb scanned him, then shut off.

Cruz always got super nervous waiting for the journal to open. He could tell he wasn't the only one. Every neck was tipped back, every eye intently fixed on the space above the journal.

"Hi, Cruzer."

Seeing his mom's holo-image, Cruz relaxed. "Hi, Mom."

"Cruz, do you have the fourth piece of the cipher?" His mom swept her long blond hair over one shoulder.

Cruz tugged on the collar of his tee, curling a finger on the lanyard he wore around his neck. Bringing it out, he unsnapped the marble from the other cipher pieces. Petra Coronado bent to examine the pie-shaped stone in her son's hand.

"I thought you gave it to Hubbard for safekeeping," whispered Sailor.

"I took it back," Cruz muttered out of the side of his mouth. "Couldn't very well leave it here over break, could I?"

"Well done," said Cruz's mom. "This is a genuine piece. You have unlocked a new clue."

"Sweet as!" called Sailor as Lani and Emmett clapped.

"To find the fifth cipher, you'll need a little help from your aunt," continued his mother. "Marisol is my best friend and has been since the day we first met at Explorer Academy. Though I have but one keepsake from her life, your aunt or your dad will have all of the odds and ends of mine. The third time's the charm if you hope to find the cipher. Good luck, Cruzer." Her image began to fade.

"That's not much to go on." Lani blew out a puff of air. "I wonder if—Cruz?"

He was already across the room, pulling an aqua-colored box from under his bed. "This is the box of my mom's stuff my aunt gave me," Cruz reminded his friends. "I think that's what Mom means about needing a little help from my aunt and the odds and ends of her life."

Emmett and Lani knelt on either side of Cruz, and Sailor hopped on the bed to peer over the edge. Cruz tossed off the lid from the box and began pawing through the contents: assorted pens and pencils, a photo of him as a kid, a pad of cat sticky notes, a box of bandages, a package of almonds tied with a red ribbon, a couple of washers, a key … Where was it?

Lani reached into the corner of the box for the photo. She flipped it over and gasped. "The swirl cipher! I've been wanting to see it in person."

"That's what started it all," said Emmett.

"Got it!" cried Cruz, reeling back.

"What?" Sailor leaned so far over the edge of the mattress she lost her balance. Fortunately, Emmett and Lani caught her before she fell on her head. Inches from Cruz's fingers she gasped. "An Aztec crown charm? Oh sure, I get it! The third time's the *charm*!"

Lani squinted. "There's something engraved on the back, but it's so tiny I can't—"

"I'll read it," said Emmett.

"Please don't tell me those glasses have x-ray vision," said Lani.

"No." Emmett's cheeks flushed. "But they do have an advanced magnification feature."

Lani did her best to hide her grin. She'd been teasing. They all knew Emmett's glasses gave him the vision of an eagle, which can spot its prey from two miles away.

Cruz handed the charm to his roommate.

"Let's see … it says NEMINARET and there's a number below it," declared Emmett. "1-1-2-9."

"Eleven twenty-nine could stand for November twenty-ninth, my birthday," said Cruz. "But what's a neminaret?"

Nobody knew. They went for their tablets to start researching.

"I'll check Aztec gods and history," said Sailor. Still on Cruz's bed, she'd tucked her legs under her so she could balance her tablet on her knees.

Lani remained on the floor. She scooted back until she was leaning against Cruz's bed frame. "I'll cover people and places."

Emmett held up a hand. "Science and education."

"I'll take reference and media," said Cruz. He searched for the term "neminaret" in the Academy library's online reference section, but could not find it in any dictionary, encyclopedia, or thesaurus. He then moved on to look under news, movies, TV, music, and games. Again, nothing. "I'm coming up empty. Are you guys finding anything?"

"No," said Emmett.

Sailor sat up. "A big nothing from me, too."

Cruz peered around the chair. "Lani?"

"I could only find on articles on minarets," said Lani. "You know, the towers that are used to call people to prayer. Did you know one of the minarets on the Taj Mahal was damaged in an earthquake?"

Sailor bent to look over the edge of Cruz's bed. "Did it fall?"

"No." Lani tipped her head back to look up at her. "But the minarets at the Taj Mahal were built tilting slightly outward, so that if they ever *do* fall, they won't damage the tomb."

"Smart," said Sailor.

"Guys," broke in Emmett. "What if NEMINARET isn't a person, place, or thing?"

"What's left?" wondered Lani.

"I was thinking a code. We know Cruz's mom used two codes, at least, to communicate with him: the swirl cipher and the rainbow cryptogram."

Cruz tipped his head. "Could it be a Caesar cipher?"

"You read my mind," said Emmett.

"What's that?" asked Sailor.

"A Caesar cipher requires you to move each letter down a certain number of positions in the alphabet in order to decode it," explained Emmett. "The most basic one is to move the letters one spot, so A becomes code for B, B is code for C, and so on, and when you get to Z—"

"Z is code for A," finished Sailor. "Got it. So, what does it spell?"

"Hold on … one … second …" Cruz was scribbling on his tablet. "O-F-N-J-O-B-S-F-U. Often jobs for you?"

That didn't sound right.

"Maybe you did it wrong," Sailor said to Cruz.

He frowned. "I don't think so …"

"We're forgetting the clue," said Lani. "The *third* time's the charm. Try shifting down three letters."

That had to be it! He quickly scrawled the alphabet in two columns on his tablet. Counting in three letters, Cruz put an A next to the D, a B beside the E, and so on.

He got Q-H-P-L-Q-D-U-H-W.

Sailor sighed. "That's even worse than the first one."

"There are too many possibilities," said Emmett. "The shift could start in the middle of the alphabet, skip certain letters, or go backward from Z."

"It could also be a totally different code," said Cruz. "Like one that substitutes *any* letter for another. Plus, with the 1-1-2-9 there, it could include numbers, too. Other than being my birthday, we don't know what it stands for."

"What you're both saying is that without a cipher we're sunk," said Lani.

Emmett's glasses turned tangerine. "Afraid so."

Sailor hung over the side of Cruz's bed. "Got any other decoders in your mom's box?"

"Nope." Cruz was tired and it was getting stuffy in the cabin.

Setting his tablet aside, Cruz got up and went to open the door to the veranda. He felt a rush of wind. Cruz looked up at the stars glittering in a black, moonless sky. He knew you could see stars more clearly once you were away from the lights of the city, and out here, in the western Indian Ocean with no land in sight, it was true. The whole sky was sparkling.

"Gotta go." Sailor had poked her head out. "Ten minutes until lights-out."

Cruz followed her back inside. Emmett was already in the bathroom, brushing his teeth. Sailor left, while Lani stayed to help Cruz put his mom's things away. They knelt by the aqua box. Cruz slipped the silver Aztec crown into the front pocket of his uniform where he kept Mell. His hand went to the opposite pocket, where he'd tucked the fourth piece of the cipher. Cruz took it out, letting the smooth, dark stone tumble from his fingers into his palm. He had come to a decision.

Cruz was not going to put the cipher back in Hubbard's life vest. It was too risky. It had been a good hiding place in the beginning, when he had only one or two sections of the circular cipher. But the more pieces he attached, the more likely it was that someone might notice the stones in Hubbard's pocket—Taryn, a professor, one of the explorers, even the spies.

The explorer spy!

Danger is closer than you know.

Remembering the warning from his mysterious friend sent a shiver down Cruz's spine. Cruz knew he needed to figure out the identity of the explorer spy. He was hoping his anonymous friend would write again with more clues. But there hadn't been anything since before winter break. There seemed no clear pattern to when, where, or how the notes appeared. The last message had come on the inside of a box and been delivered along with his clean uniform; very different from the first letter, which had arrived via regular mail and had a postmark from London, England. Mystery friend's identity was as baffling as that of the spy.

Cruz hadn't told his dad or aunt about the explorer spy. He'd also kept it from his friends. Lani, of course, wasn't the culprit. They had known each other forever. She would never betray him; however, she might accidentally let it slip to Sailor and Emmett that someone among them was a spy. Cruz didn't believe his friends were Nebula agents either, but he had to be sure. The problem was, how?

Lani placed the lid back on his mom's box. Cruz saw she was staring at the stone in his hand. "What?" he asked.

"I don't know ... I was thinking, it's weird how something so little ..." She stopped.

"Could be worth someone's life?" he dared to finish.

Cruz had often thought the same thing. This was the first time, however, he'd said it out loud. His own words slit him like a paper cut— quickly yet sharply.

"Cruz, I'm ... I'm sorry," stammered Lani. "I shouldn't have said that. I didn't mean—"

"It's okay, *hoaaloha*," whispered Cruz, but he had tears in his eyes. So did she.

5

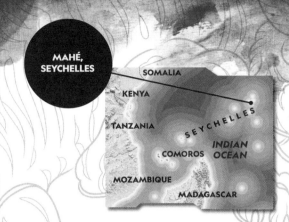

MAHÉ, SEYCHELLES

SOMALIA
KENYA
TANZANIA
SEYCHELLES
COMOROS
INDIAN OCEAN
MOZAMBIQUE
MADAGASCAR

▶**GOOD MORNING,** *explorer!*

*While you were dreaming, Orion arrived in the inner islands of the Seychelles. We are now anchored off Mahé, the largest of the archipelago's 115 islands and home to the capital city of Victoria. Your next mission is unlike any expedition we have done so far. You will need to be flexible and industrious. Report to the CAVE at 8:00 this morning as a **complete team** for a briefing. You will not be admitted until all team members are present. Prepare for warm yet rainy weather. Wear sunscreen. Bring your camera, tablet, and water in your backpack. Dare to Explore!*

Professor B. Gabriel

"*Mōrena.*" Sailor's breakfast tray landed next to Cruz's on the table. "We've got a problem."

A second earlier, Cruz had stuck a bite of the fluffiest blueberry pancakes on Earth into his mouth, so it was up to his roommate to respond.

"I know," said Emmett. "Can you believe they ran out of sausage that fast?"

"That's not what I meant." Turning to Cruz, Sailor flicked her head back toward the buffet line. "I meant your crush."

Cruz nearly choked. "My ... my what?"

"Might as well fess up. It's common knowledge from bow to stern. You're keen on her. She thinks you're the ant's pants."

Cruz looked at Emmett for confirmation. His roommate gave a rapid nod, and Cruz felt a rush of blood in his cheeks. He reached for his orange juice.

Sailor slid into her seat. "Did you pash yet?"

Was this a Maori word, too? More Kiwi slang? Gulping juice, Cruz lifted his eyebrows.

"Pash!" Sailor threw her head back. "Kiss, man, kiss!"

Cruz nearly spit out his juice all over Emmett. "We . . . I . . ." he sputtered.

Again, he looked to Emmett, but his friend was clearly enjoying this. His emoto-glasses looked like shaken soda pop in a cartoon: bright lime circles brimming with pink and blue bubbles.

"Fill me in later, she's almost to the end of the line," said Sailor. "Look, Bryndis knows Lani and I go to your cabin to work on 'the puzzle.'" She made air quotes. "She's been hinting she wants to know what's going on, and I'm running out of excuses. I hate lying to my best friend. I don't care what you do—make up a story, tell her the truth—but please do *something*."

"Okay," said Cruz. "I will."

Sailor was right. He *had* left Bryndis hanging. He'd told her bits of information about the search for his mom's formula but never the full story. It was only natural for her to be curious. She deserved more than partial explanations, but the question was, how much more? Could he trust Bryndis? If the answer was no, he shouldn't be . . . She shouldn't be . . . Well, they shouldn't *be*, right? His head felt as mushy as the syrup-soaked pancakes on his plate. He would have to sort this out later. At the moment, Cruz had a more pressing matter on his mind.

On their way to breakfast, Cruz and Emmett had stopped by the lab to see Fanchon as she'd requested. The tech lab chief had been studying data on a PANDA unit that had been found during Cruz's DNA analysis of one of the cipher pieces. The handheld Portable Artifact Notation and Data Analyzer had projected a brief video snippet of his mom reading her laboratory logbook. However, only part of the log entry was visible. Fanchon offered to run it through her state-of-the-art software to see if she could recover more of it.

"Fanchon must have good news." Emmett had punched Cruz's shoulder as they hurried to the lab. "Why else would she want to see you?"

Cruz agreed, but the moment he saw Fanchon's face, his hopes faded.

"I was able to capture a little more of the entry, but there was only so much I could do." Fanchon wiped her hands on the hem of a pink apron with a cookie print that read *Scientists Are Smart Cookies.* "It's old technology, the depth of field is shallow, your mom's shoulder has this weird glow to it that's interfering with things, and I have a bunch more excuses you don't want to hear. Anyway, have a look." She tapped her screen and the holo-video of Cruz's mom reading her logbook appeared in the cubicle. Freezing the image, Fanchon highlighted the new words:

> *cell regeneration has remarkable potential, **but my error***
> *when I handled the **serum I didn't notice the cut on my wrist.***
> ***and for now** it appears that Cruz is, too.*
> *the full power of the **serum will not kick in***
> *could change his entire life. **I am unsure***
> *but I know I must find a way.*
> *How do you begin to tell your son **his destiny may be***

It wasn't earth-shattering, but there *was* some new information. His mom wrote she'd been cut. Had the serum hurt her in some way? If so, she hadn't mentioned anything about it in her holo-journal messages to him. Why had she been unsure? Was she trying to make the serum safer? Had something gone wrong? And what about the last sentence? *How do you begin to tell your son his destiny may be . . .*

What?

. . . to lose me?

. . . to hunt for my formula?

. . . to die at the hands of Nebula?

It could be a hundred things!

Beside him, Emmett was also carefully inspecting the image, his emoto-glasses in flux. Cruz watched the frames morph from a thoughtful pale blue to lavender to deep purple. The color and shape, trapezoids with soft corners, told him Emmett was suspicious. Or worried. Maybe both.

"See something?" prodded Cruz.

Emmett clicked his tongue. "Is your mom in her lab here?"

"Uh . . . I think so." Cruz had assumed she was but didn't know for certain. Everything behind the logbook was out of focus. He could see a long dark boxlike shape and a tall blue blob.

"I can try to enhance the background." Fanchon bent over her touch screen.

"What is it?" Cruz whispered to Emmett.

Emmett shook his head. "Not sure."

A few minutes later, Fanchon straightened. "This is the best I can do. Any better?"

It was. They could now tell that the block was a row of books lined up inside a glass case. The blue blob was a bit sharper but still not distinguishable.

"That could be a lamp," guessed Cruz.

Fanchon tilted her head. "If it is, it's an awfully big one."

"It's got a triangle on the front." Cruz squinted at the three black lines creating a slanted pyramid. "I think." He turned to his roommate, who had better vision—eight times better than the average human, thanks to his glasses.

Emmett, however, was no longer next to him.

"Uh … Emmett?" called Cruz, spinning.

"We'd better go," said Emmett from outside the cubicle. "It's seven twenty and we still need to eat."

"He's right," Cruz said to Fanchon. "It's a mission day. Plus, those cookies on your apron are making me hungry."

She laughed. "Sugar cookies—they're the best."

"Double chocolate chip for me," said Cruz. "Thanks, Fanchon."

"You're welcome. I wish I could have been more helpful. Maybe in the future we'll have the technology to reveal more of the entry."

"Maybe. Anything's possible, right?"

Cruz had to jog to catch up to his roommate, who was barreling through the cubicles like a cheetah. "Emmett, wait up."

At the door, Emmett turned and a pair of brilliant white trapezoids blinded Cruz.

"Whoa!" Cruz threw up a hand.

Emmett ripped off his glasses and the white inside the frames broke apart like a snow flurry. In 10 seconds, the glasses had returned to lime ovals. Emmett's frames didn't go white very often. It meant an overload of emotions, like a surge of electricity shorting a circuit.

"What's going on?" whispered Cruz.

Sliding the frames back onto his nose, Emmett looked around. "What if I told you your mom's logbook might not have been destroyed in the lab fire . . . that it still might exist?"

Cruz's mouth dropped open. "How do you know?"

"When Fanchon fixed the background, I could read the titles on the book spines. I saw *De Revolutionibus Orbium Coelestium* by Nicolaus Copernicus."

"Huh?"

"It means *On the Revolutions of Heavenly Spheres.* See, in the sixteenth century, Copernicus was one of the first scientists to say that the Earth revolved around the sun and not the other way around. And the book next to that was *On the Origin of Species* by Charles Darwin, then *Relativity* by Albert Einstein and *Dialogue Concerning the Two Chief World Systems* by Galileo . . ." Emmett was talking faster and faster. "They looked like *first* editions, but I couldn't be sure . . ."

"Of what?" Cruz didn't understand what old books had to do with anything.

Emmett was still rambling. ". . . until I saw the blurry blue shapes. They looked like the buses the curators wear."

Cruz was totally lost. "Buses?"

"*B-U-S-S.* It stands for Bioluminescent Universal Safety Suit."

"Suit? You think the blue glowy thing is a person?" quizzed Cruz.

Emmett nodded. "I wasn't positive until I saw the triangle on the jumpsuit, which isn't a triangle at all, by the way. It's an A . . . the letter A, Cruz."

Their eyes met. Goose bumps tumbled down Cruz's arms. "A as in . . . Archive?"

Emmett, finally, took a breath. "Yes."

"My mom's logbook is in the Archive?" Cruz couldn't believe it. He had to say it again. "My mom's logbook is in the Archive!"

"Might be," cautioned his friend.

"Might be," echoed Cruz. He needed a minute to let that sink in. "Okay. We know the Archive is in the basement of the Academy, so now all we have to do is figure out—"

"Cruz, you don't—"

"I doubt Aunt Marisol can help us. She let it slip once, about the Archive, and totally freaked out—told me to forget I'd ever heard her say it." He tapped his chin. "And if she won't admit the place exists, I'm pretty sure neither will Dr. Hightower or any of the faculty ... Hey, what about your mom?"

"She doesn't have clearance," said Emmett. "Only a handful of people in the world do. It's one level above top secret."

"There's a level above top secret? What's it called?"

Emmett gave him an exasperated look.

"Right," said Cruz. "Of course. It's top secret."

This *was* going to be a challenge.

"We shouldn't be talking about this here." Emmett reached for the doorknob.

"Hold on." Cruz had asked his roommate once before about the Archive but had never gotten an answer. Now he needed one. "If the Archive is so secret that not even your mom has clearance, how do *you* know about the BUSSs? How do you know the vault contains stuff like ..." He tried to remember all the impressive items Emmett had told him were there. "... the original Gettysburg Address and the 'Mona Lisa' ... and ... and the formula for Pepsi?"

"Coke," corrected Emmett. "But Pepsi's probably in there, too."

Cruz shot him an I'm-in-no-mood glare.

"It's because ... Okay, I might know someone who does have clearance."

"Well, your mom works for the Synthesis, so it must be your dad, right?" joked Cruz.

Emmett's glasses went from a cloudy maroon to a truthful bright pink.

Cruz was stunned. "He does? Seriously? Your dad works in the Archive?"

"Shhh-shhh!" Emmett's head swiveled left, then right. "If anyone knew, he could lose his job."

Cruz's eyes narrowed. "What are you guys, like Super Spy Family or something?"

It was Emmett's turn to glare.

That's when it hit Cruz. He knew how to discover if Emmett was Nebula's explorer spy. The answer was so simple! It had been in front him the whole time. Literally.

Cruz leaned toward his front. "Emmett, are you a spy for Nebula?"

"*What?*" Emmett's emoto-frames turned an even deeper shade of pink.

Emmett might be able to lie, but his glasses couldn't. He was no spy.

"Just checking," said Cruz.

"Did you say you were just checking? You're kidding, right? I'm your closest friend at the Academy." Little orange streaks were now pulsing through the emoto-frames. Emmett's nostrils were flaring, too. "What would make you think—"

Cruz put a hand on Emmett's arm. "Sorry. I'll explain later. You'll ask your dad about the logbook?"

"Yeah, but even if he finds it, it won't matter. He's not allowed to tell you what's in it."

"Why not?"

"Because that's how it works." Emmett rubbed his forehead. "It's not a public library or museum, Cruz. It's a highly secure, climate-controlled, supersecret mega-vault—"

"I know, but your dad wouldn't say no to his own son—"

"He already has," barked Emmett. "That's what I've been trying to tell you. Trust me when I say the logbook may be in the Archive, but you and me?" Brown eyes widened behind a pair of swirling pink-and-orange frames. "We'll never get within an inch of it."

6

►MONSIEUR LEGRAND

was standing at the entrance to the CAVE when Team Cousteau arrived at seven minutes before eight o'clock. His jaw was set, arms folded. Their fitness and survival training instructor was not alone. Kat, Tao, Ali, Yulia, and Zane—five of the six members of Team Magellan—were there, too.

Cruz assessed the situation pretty quickly. The instructions from Professor Gabriel had been clear: No team would be allowed to enter the Computer Animated Virtual Experience until *all* members were present. Matteo was missing. And Monsieur Legrand wasn't about to let anyone break the rules.

Cruz, who was in the lead for Cousteau, could have taken his team past Magellan's into the CAVE. Instead, he stopped behind Zane and gave him a questioning eyebrow.

Zane rolled his eyes. "Matteo left his MC camera at breakfast. Guess you guys want to go ahead of us, huh?"

Cruz *did* want to go in, but it didn't seem fair to cut in front of Magellan. They were here first. And as long as no one was late for the mission assignment, would it really make a difference what order they entered the CAVE?

Cruz glanced back at his teammates. "You guys don't mind if we wait, do you?"

46

"I do." Dugan was shooing Cruz forward. "It could be a competition. We don't want to be last."

"Dugan's right," said Emmett. "Professor Ishikawa must have had a reason for telling us to enter as a team. Maybe we should go ahead."

"I'm here! I'm here!" Matteo was jogging down the passage. He made his way past Team Cousteau, avoiding eye contact, to join his team. Once he had, Monsieur Legrand waved Magellan into the CAVE. Zane turned, giving Cruz a grateful smile.

The line began to move.

"*Bonjour*, Zane," said Monsieur Legrand. He handed him a white cube about twice the size of a child's building block.

"Uh ... thanks?" Zane glanced at Cruz, who lifted a shoulder as if to say he had no idea what it was either, then entered the CAVE.

"*Bonjour*, Cruz," said their fitness instructor.

"*Bonjour*, Monsieur Legrand," said Cruz.

Instead of handing him a cube, too, his teacher whispered, *"Tout est vu."* He said it so quietly, the translator on Cruz's comm pin didn't catch it.

Cruz stepped into the CAVE. "Translator to lowest volume," he muttered, then repeated Monsieur Legrand's phrase as best as he could. *"Tout est vu."*

"Everything is seen," said the translator.

Cruz saw Monsieur Legrand give Lani, the last person in line for Cousteau, a white cube like Zane's. They were the final team in. Without a word, the group headed across the big, dark compartment to where the rest of the explorers had formed a semicircle around Professor Gabriel. Cory from Team Galileo and Kendall with Team Earhart were also holding cubes.

Professor Gabriel welcomed them. "As I mentioned in my note, your next mission is unlike any we've done so far. Because this area is home to so many rare plant and animal species, we want to extend our reach as far as possible. Instead of a single task that you will do together, every team will be assigned a unique project."

Around them, each of the four tall walls of the CAVE transformed into a different holo-scene! There was a coral reef, a tropical beach, a palm forest, and a cave.

"Whoa!" Cruz whirled, trying to take it all in.

Everyone else was spinning, too.

"Project One." Their professor motioned behind him to the underwater scene. Several silvery yellow angelfish glided through the teal waters. They swam past a series of ropes stretched out across the reef like clotheslines. Small chunks of bumpy brown coral were attached to the ropes—one clump of coral every few inches.

"You are peering into a coral nursery," said a female voice Cruz knew well.

Aunt Marisol! She stepped into the light next to Professor Gabriel, wearing a white shirt with the sleeves rolled up and khaki pants. She'd piled her dark hair up into a loose bun on top of her head. "You've learned that coral and algae have a symbiotic relationship, and that warming ocean temperatures, pollution, and other factors can cause the algae to leave the coral. Without its major food source, which also provides its color, the coral turns white, or bleaches. Coral can survive bleaching for a while, but if sea conditions don't improve, it will die. Several bleaching events this century have harmed the coral colonies in the Seychelles." She lifted a hand, her charm bracelet sliding toward her elbow. "Here in the nursery, rescued coral fragments are protected as they grow, then they're transplanted onto damaged reefs. In Project Reef Rescue, I will lead a dive team to a nursery off Silhouette island. We'll check on the corals, clean the nursery, and move any mature corals that are ready to become a permanent part of the reef that encircles the island."

Cruz nudged Bryndis. "Remember your Halloween costume?" She had come to the party dressed as bleached coral.

"What was I thinking?" She shook her head. "I looked like a yogurt-covered pretzel."

"You looked great," he said, which got a grin out of her.

Sailor was tapping his arm. "I know your aunt's a diver because of her marine archaeology background but I didn't know she was into reef conservation."

"Oh yeah," answered Cruz. "She's spent the last few summers helping with coral restoration in the Great Barrier Reef."

"Really? I would love to do that."

"You should ask her about it."

"I will," vowed Sailor.

"Project Two." Professor Gabriel's voice boomed through the compartment. Their instructor moved toward the wall to his left where the gentle, foamy surf spilled onto an empty beach. Cruz heard the sound of palm leaves fluttering in the wind a second before he felt it ruffle his hair.

"Ohhh!" It was Weatherly, the explorer closest to that wall. Leaning forward, Cruz saw Weatherly bend to touch a domed gray shell. A giant holo-tortoise! A stocky neck was stretching up to get a better look at her, too.

"Found only in the Seychelles, the Aldabra giant tortoise is one of the largest tortoises in the world." Professor Ishikawa appeared from the shadows. "At one time, there were several types of giant tortoises in this region, but most were hunted to extinction for their shells and meat. The Aldabra tortoise nearly suffered the same fate. Fortunately, the government stepped in to protect the tortoise, thanks to the efforts of naturalist Charles Darwin and other concerned scientists of his time. It was one of the first species in the world to be protected by law. Now you'll find more than a hundred thousand of these tortoises living on the Aldabra Atoll in the outer islands, as well as healthy populations on many of the other islands, like Mahé. Even so, this species is still at risk from poachers and predators, who raid the nests for eggs." Their biology teacher strolled to the holo-tortoise and knelt next to it. "In Project Tortoise and Turtle Watch, I will lead a team to tag and release young hatchlings and monitor nesting sites. Also, the Seychelles is home to one of the largest remaining hawksbill turtle populations on Earth. Since it is nearing the end of breeding season, the first batch of babies should soon be hatching. We'll check on some of the sea turtle nesting sites, because they, too, are at risk."

Cruz tugged on Emmett's sleeve. "What a great chance to try out the EggsTend!"

His roommate's glasses were flashing gold. "It *is* ready."

"We have to get this one for Emmett," Cruz whispered to Bryndis. "His Funday group made an egg robot to monitor sea turtle nests."

She nodded. "Let's see if we can get it."

Professor Gabriel was on the move again. This time, he strolled to the wall opposite the beach to the cave scene. Cruz could see a circle of light in the distance and got a whiff of a strong, musty smell. He heard flapping. A swarm of large insects was flying through the tunnel, straight for them. At first, Cruz thought they were big grasshoppers. As they closed in, he realized he was wrong. They were small bats! Everyone ducked and the colony flew over their heads, circling to land on a craggy ledge jutting out from the cave wall.

"Ew," squeaked Bryndis.

"Cool," gasped Lani.

A light came on under the roost, revealing Professor Kira Benedict, the explorers' journalism teacher. "This winged mammal is known as a sheath-tailed bat," she said. "Like the Aldabra tortoise, this species of bat is found nowhere else on Earth. Sadly, this creature is not doing nearly as well as the tortoise. With fewer than one hundred left, the sheath-tailed bat is on the brink of extinction. We can help the bats by protecting their forest habitat and reducing pesticide use. However, the world won't know this remarkable animal is in trouble unless we tell them, which is why I will be leading Bats on the Brink, a project to photo-graph the sheath-tailed bats and share their story before it's too late."

Cruz wanted to get a look at the small, winged rodents clinging to the stone wall, but Professor Gabriel was already strolling toward the jungle on the back wall. The canopy of palms and broadleaf trees was thick; their branches blocked much of the sun. What light could get through was separated into thin beams of haze. Thick bushes, ferns, and dead palm leaves covered the ground. Cruz watched a rat skitter past, the sun dappling its back.

"Project Four," said their teacher. "In my class, you've learned that an invasive species is a plant or animal that is not native to an area, which upsets the balance of that ecosystem. Coconut palms are indige-nous to the Seychelles but are only meant to grow on the outer rim of an island, leaving the hardwood forest inland to support bird life. However, in the mid-nineteenth century, people began cutting down the hardwood trees so they could plant coconut and cinnamon trees instead. The coconuts were harvested for oil, and you know, of course, that cinnamon is a popular spice. These trees spread, crowding out the native species." A cute brownish green songbird landed on a branch next to Sailor and began to tweet. "Due to the loss of their nesting trees, birds like the Seychelles warbler here nearly went extinct," continued Professor Gabriel. "Fortunately, in the twentieth century, conservation teams focused their efforts on removing invasive plants and bird populations began to recover. I will be leading Project Habitat Help. Along with a local conservation team, we'll be removing invasive species and planting native growth..."

"That sounds a lot like gardening," whispered Bryndis.

"That's because it is," said Sailor.

"Who would want to do that?"

"Not me," said Dugan.

"Odds are in our favor that we won't have to," whispered Emmett.

"It's actually kind of fun," said Lani. "Back home, Cr—I mean, I helped with a habitat restoration project on Mauna Kea." She gave Cruz an apologetic grimace. They were keeping it a secret that they had known each other before coming to the Academy so no one would think Lani had gotten special treatment from Dr. Hightower.

"There you have it, explorers!" boomed Professor Gabriel. "Your four projects. Once you have your assignments, you are to immediately report to aquatics. Jaz will take each team ashore in the tender boat.

We have a lot to accomplish in a short amount of time, so we'll be choosing teams quickly—no games or contests today."

A chorus of moans echoed through the CAVE.

"When you entered the CAVE this morning, Monsieur Legrand gave one member from each team a cube," said Professor Gabriel.

Lani, Zane, Cory, and Kendall held up their blocks.

Team Cousteau huddled around Lani, who was balancing the square on her palm. Inside it, a smoky substance swirled like storm clouds.

"In a few moments, a reef, beach, cave, or jungle will be revealed within your cube," said their teacher. "The holo-scene you see will be your team's project."

"Come on, beach," rooted Cruz. They had to get Project Tortoise and Turtle Watch for Emmett. "Beach, beach, beach..."

Bryndis joined in. "Beach, beach..."

Then Sailor and Lani. "Beach, beach..."

Dugan began his own chant. "Anything but the jungle, anything but the jungle..."

That made them giggle.

The fog inside their cube was starting to clear. Cruz held his breath. He saw palm trees! There was something greenish toward the middle. Surf? The mist was taking forever to dissolve. Cruz couldn't wait for his first glimpse of the shoreline.

Come on, beach, come on...

"It's sand!" whooped Cruz.

"It's dirt," wailed Dugan.

He was right. Team Cousteau was staring at a miniature tropical forest. They'd gotten Project Habitat Help. Ugh.

Nearby, Team Earhart was all smiles, watching a coral reef slosh inside their square. Team Galileo was celebrating, too, as they gazed into a small, dark cavern. Stretching his neck, Cruz saw that Zane's block contained the sandy shore Cousteau had wanted. Ali, Tao, Yulia, Kat, and Matteo were slapping Zane on the back like he was the star athlete who'd led them to victory.

"What did you guys get?" asked Felipe.

"We got Habitat Help," said Sailor. "We're super excited. It's going to be so awesome!" She said it too loudly and with too much energy. Emmett and Bryndis tried to pretend they were thrilled too, but they were worse actors than Sailor. It didn't help that Emmett's emoto-glasses were the color of mud.

"It'll be okay, you'll all see," said Lani softly. "It's a good project."

"Thanks," mouthed Cruz. He knew she was trying to cheer him up. It didn't work.

Cruz felt awful. He didn't need anyone to tell him that had Team Cousteau gone ahead of Magellan into the CAVE, *they* would have gotten the beach cube and *they* would be doing the tortoise and turtle project. But Dugan did anyway.

Many times.

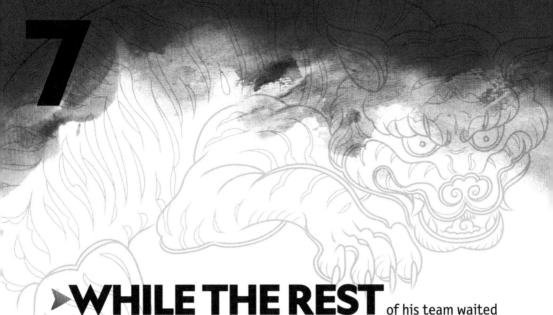

7

▶**WHILE THE REST** of his team waited inside aquatics with the other explorers, Cruz had wandered outside to the rail, then down a flight of stairs to the lower aft deck. He needed a minute alone. He knew how his teammates would react to his error. Bryndis would be encouraging; Sailor, funny; Lani, practical; Emmett, kind; and Dugan, honest. Brutally honest.

Cruz absently strolled under the stairs. Through the slats between the steps, he watched Jaz and a couple of deckhands prepare *Orion*'s tender boat, *Rigel*, for departure.

There was only enough room on the small hovercraft for eight people. The plan was for Jaz to transport the teams one by one. Magellan was first on Jaz's schedule. They would be making a quick trip across the bay to Mahé Island. Team Cousteau was also headed to the island and would go second. Teams Galileo and Earhart were slotted in the third and fourth positions, because they had the farthest to travel. Both were bound for the island of Silhouette, about 12 miles northwest of Mahé.

Cruz heard footsteps. And voices. People were coming down the stairs.

"Did you remember your MC camera?" It was Ali.

Wanting to avoid Ali, Cruz stepped back deeper into the shadows of the staircase.

"Yep," said Matteo. "Don't worry. I wouldn't dare forget it again."

"I can't wait to see the hatchlings," said Zane.

"Me too," said Zane. "Although …" His foot stopped on the step directly in front of Cruz's face.

Cruz inched back until he felt a pipe dig into his shoulder blade.

One step up, Ali and Matteo paused. "What?" asked Matteo.

"I feel kinda bad for Team Cousteau," finished Zane.

Ali grunted. "They could have gone ahead of us. It's not like we blocked them from going into the CAVE or anything."

"I know," said Zane. "Cruz was being nice. Maybe we should have offered to trade projects with them."

"Trade?" cried Ali. "Are you kidding? You want to do Project Yard Work?"

"No-oo-oo!"

"Then chill. And besides, Cruz isn't *that* nice."

More footsteps. And voices. "Did everyone remember their water and sunscreen?" It was Professor Ishikawa. The rest of Team Magellan came trotting down the steps with him.

Ali's words had stung Cruz. He hoped Zane knew him better than that. He also hoped Zane wouldn't be influenced by his teammate, but he probably would be. After all, there was a connection that formed between the members of an Explorer Academy team that went beyond friendship. You relied on them to get through missions. Trusted their judgment. Formed a bond. Cruz had seen it happen within his own team.

Rigel's engine was starting. From his hiding place, Cruz watched Jaz fling a rope to a deckhand. A minute later, the black, oval hovercraft backed away from the ship. It rose out of the water and made a smooth, easy turn. The boat skimmed the tops of the waves as it sped toward a curved beach guarded by chunks of black granite. Mountains towered over coast, their slopes covered with thick jungles. Professor Gabriel had told Team Cousteau they would be hiking into the mountains for their mission. Cruz's eyes traveled up to the lazy clouds that hid the peaks. He wondered how high they'd be going.

"There you are!"

Whirling, Cruz smacked his elbow on a post and a tingling spasm of pain shot down his left arm. He grabbed his left elbow with his right hand, hugging it to him. "Lani!"

"Hit your funny bone, huh? Give it here." Lani reached out to rub the sting from his elbow. "I've been looking everywhere for you. You don't have to hide out like a criminal, you know."

"I wasn't hiding," he muttered. "I was . . . taking a break."

Lani glanced around. "Uh-huh." She wasn't buying it.

Cruz sighed. "If I had gone ahead of Magellan into the CAVE—"

"I *still* could have gotten the same cube," insisted Lani. "Monsieur Legrand might have decided which team got which cube before we ever got there."

Cruz had never considered that. "Maybe, but Emmett's EggsTend—"

"Will be deployed," she said. "Kat's going to do it, once Professor Ishikawa gets the green light from the conservation center. Kat was on Emmett's robotics team, and it's her project as much as it is his."

Good ole practical Lani. Cruz could always count on her to think through all the angles.

Lani released his arm. Only his fingertips still tingled. "Come up with the rest of us. Otherwise, Professor Gabriel is going to think you don't want to go on the mission."

Cruz didn't want to hurt his teacher's feelings. Lani was right. What was done was done. Moping wasn't going to change anything. Besides, he had something important to discuss with his best friend, and he didn't want to wait until after the mission. Peeking through the steps, he could see that *Rigel* was almost to the dock at Mahé. It wouldn't be long before Jaz would be on her way back. "Lani, I have to—"

"Cruz, I need to—"

Both had started talking at once.

They laughed.

"Sorry!" Cruz and Lani said in unison.

"You go first," said Lani.

Cruz took a breath. "Emmett is the only one who knows what I'm about to tell you. I haven't said a word to my dad, Aunt Marisol, or even Sailor." He lowered his voice to a whisper. "Remember my anonymous friend? The one who warned me about Nebula . . . ?"

Lani gasped. "You got another message!"

"Uh-huh. It came a while ago. Before break. The note said Nebula has a spy on board *Orion* and . . . it's an explorer."

"Nooooo!" She drew back. "Although it would explain why Nebula always seems to magically know where you're going and what you're doing."

"The note said, 'Danger is closer than you think.' I think the sender is trying to tell me the spy is one of my friends or teammates."

"Whoa! I wonder who it could be?"

"I don't know. And until I do—"

"Everyone's a suspect."

"Except Emmett," said Cruz. "Thanks to his emoto-glasses, he's the one person I could ask straight out. And I did. He's not the agent."

"Emmett does wear his heart on his glasses, doesn't he?" Lani bit her lip. "If only we could make a pair of emoto-glasses for everyone in class, we'd smoke out the spy in no time."

"I wish," said Cruz. "That's my problem. With so many suspects, how do I figure out who's the agent?"

"Only one way I know to catch a spy." Lani edged closer, directly into a strip of sunlight that had slipped between the steps. The beam lit up her eyes like a golden mask. "Set a trap."

Did they dare? It was risky. They'd have to be extremely careful. If the spy caught on to their plan and tipped off Nebula, it could be disastrous. On the other hand, if they succeeded, they'd get the jump on Nebula and maybe even give Cruz the crucial lead he needed to find the rest of the cipher.

"Professor Gabriel to Cruz Coronado and Lani Kealoha."

The voice blaring through their comm pins gave Cruz a jolt. He tapped his pin. "Cruz, here. Lani's with me, Professor Gabriel. We're on the lower deck."

"Please join your team upstairs for important departure instructions."

"On our way. Cruz, out."

Lani ducked around the post to go out the side of the stairwell.

"Hey!" Cruz called. "What were *you* going to tell *me*?"

She shot him a mischievous grin. "I figured out your mom's clue."

"*What?*"

She pointed up. "Shouldn't we—"

"Lani!"

"Okay, okay. Did you happen to notice this morning in the CAVE that your aunt was wearing a charm bracelet?"

"She always wears jewel—" He stopped, her words sinking in. "Her charm bracelet!" She hadn't worn it in a while and Cruz had forgotten all about it.

"There's more. The second charm is missing."

"It is?" Cruz's mind began to spin. "You think that's what Mom meant when she said she had a keepsake from Aunt Marisol's life?"

"Yep. I think the Aztec crown charm belongs to your aunt and when your mom said to keep in mind the old saying that the third time's the charm, she was telling you—"

"To look at the third charm on my aunt's bracelet," cried Cruz. "So, what is it? What's the third charm?"

"I don't know!" Lani balled her hands. "I got close enough to see that the second charm was missing and then we were dismissed from the CAVE. When I saw Dr. C in aquatics she wasn't wearing the bracelet anymore. She must have taken it off for the reef dive. She was busy with her team, which is why I came to find you. I thought maybe you could pull her aside and ask her *before* we have to leave on our mission—"

"Come on!" Cruz grabbed her by the wrist.

They took off.

Running up the steps with Lani, Cruz sneaked a glance out at the bay. *Rigel* was flying over the waves on its way back to *Orion*. They only had a few minutes. Once inside aquatics, Cruz put on the brakes. The explorers and faculty, along with all of their gear, were spread out across the compartment.

"Cruz! Lani!" Professor Gabriel called from his right.

Cruz spotted Kwento, Shristine, Femi, and the rest of Team Earhart—the team Aunt Marisol was leading—to his left. But he didn't see his aunt.

"Go!" Lani was pushing Cruz to the left. "I'll tell him you're coming."

Cruz charged left, trying not to trip over any explorers or their packs as his wove his way to Team Earhart. "My aunt . . . where is she?" he huffed.

Femi glanced up from folding her scuba suit. "Um . . . she was here."

"I think she went to get Seth a new pair of dive gloves," said Kwento.

Oh, great! The passage to the equipment room was on the other side of the compartment, next to where Team Cousteau had gathered. Cruz could see Sailor, Emmett, Lani, Bryndis, and Dugan clustered around Professor Gabriel. Cruz was missing important instructions. Slapping his comm pin, Cruz called his aunt. She answered right away.

"Where are you?" he asked.

"In the equipment room, helping one of the explorers."

"I have to talk to you," hissed Cruz.

"I'll only be a few minutes."

Cruz's teammates had broken out of their huddle. They were picking up their backpacks. Cousteau was getting ready to go! Lani was carrying both her pack and Cruz's as the team headed to the door. Sailor was on her toes, waving for Cruz.

"Aunt Marisol, I *really* need to talk to you," pleaded Cruz.

"Uh . . . well, Cruz, I am *with someone.*"

Bending his head toward his comm pin, Cruz cupped his hand over his mouth. "It's about your charm bracelet. What is the third charm?"

"Sorry, you're breaking up. What did you say?"

"I said 'the third charm.' I need to know—" Cruz froze. A pair of hiking boots had appeared in front of his. He lifted his head, only to peer into the narrow eyes and tight jaw of his conservation professor. Professor Gabriel lifted an eyebrow in that way adults do when they are waiting for an explanation. Dropping his hand, Cruz gulped hard. "N-never mind."

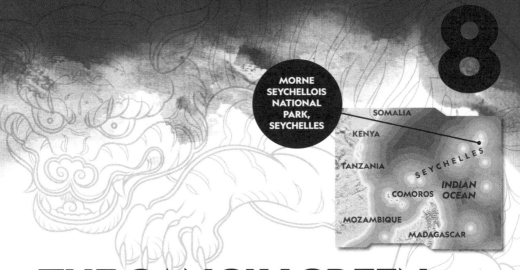

MORNE SEYCHELLOIS NATIONAL PARK, SEYCHELLES

SOMALIA
KENYA
TANZANIA
SEYCHELLES
INDIAN OCEAN
COMOROS
MOZAMBIQUE
MADAGASCAR

8

►THE GANGLY GREEN beast

was a foot taller than Cruz and twice as wide. The odds may have been stacked against him, but Cruz wasn't about to give up. Getting into a deep squat, Cruz readied himself for battle. "Let's do this!"

"Cruz?" called Sailor. "Do you need help taking out that coco plum bush?"

"I got it!"

Professor Gabriel had said one of the adults would take care of the large evergreen shrub, but Cruz had already dug a circle several feet deep around it. All that was left was to pry the thing out, and Cruz could handle that. He wrapped both gloves firmly around the trunk of the coco plum. Sinking into his heels, he began to tug. He could hear roots ripping away from soil. Suddenly, pain ripped through his biceps. Cruz didn't care if his bones crumbled. He was not about to surrender. He pulled with all his might. "Grrrrrr!"

A second later he was flat on

his back under the shrub. Victory over the leaf monster was his! He heard applause (Sailor and Lani, he guessed) and a wolf whistle (Dugan, he knew). Cruz lay there, his chest heaving. He tasted leaves. And salt. And dirt.

Was this day over yet?

Once Jaz had ferried Team Cousteau to the island that morning, they had been met at the pier by Dr. Rafi Chavreau of Seychelles Botanical Society and a handful of conservationists. From there, it was a short drive to Morne Seychellois National Park, a sprawling habitat of mangrove forests, cascading rivers, and granite mountains. Cruz's GPS informed him the park made up one-fifth of the island! After a break for snacks and water, they'd begun their hike up Morne Seychellois, the tallest peak in Seychelles.

An older man with a white beard curling over his jaw, Dr. Chavreau was celery stalk thin. Still, Cruz could barely keep up with the energetic botanist, who led them up the steep mountain terrain at a leg-burning, heart-pounding, lung-collapsing pace. After trekking more than three-quarters of the way up the mountain, they arrived at the slope where Dr. Chavreau's team had started removing invasive plants a few weeks earlier. The view was incredible. From between the tall granite boulders at the cliff's edge, Cruz could see the entire northwestern part of the coast. The shoreline jutted out from the island like a big lobster claw. He even spotted *Orion* anchored out past the entrance to the bay!

The adults used axes and chainsaws to cut down the larger trees and bushes, while the explorers dug out smaller plants and ground cover by hand. It was slow, dirty, and difficult work. Cruz had a feeling that if his teammates weren't mad at him before they started, they certainly would be once they finished—*if* they ever finished.

Shoving the coco plum off himself, Cruz sat up. He reached for his water bottle and gulped cold liquid until he had to take a breath.

A few feet away, Sailor was wrestling with the world's thickest creeping vine. She tugged at its base. It didn't budge. She pulled harder. Still nothing. Sailor gave the tendril a good yank. It snapped.

Sailor stumbled backward and came up holding a long, stringy stem but no roots. She ripped off her gardening gloves. "This is a thousand times worse than pulling weeds at my uncle's, and I get paid for that."

Dugan peered around a tree. "Vine: one; Sailor: nothing!"

Along with Lani, Dugan was ringbarking a grove of young cinnamon trees. The pair was peeling off a two-foot band of bark around the circumference of each trunk. Dr. Chavreau had shown them how to carve the outer layer away with their laser cutters, explaining that ringbarking cuts off a tree's food supply, which would ultimately lead to its death.

"Do we *have* to kill them?" Lani had quietly asked Dr. Chavreau.

"To restore the habitat, I'm afraid so," he'd answered.

Lani had done as instructed but, as always, in her own way. Cruz could hear her comforting her first victim as she cut away a ribbon of bark. "Sorry about this, but there's too many of you. We need to plant some native trees to bring back the birds and butterflies..."

"Team Cousteau!" Emmett was marching around a hairpin turn in the trail. Bryndis was with him. Each was carrying a large rectangular tray.

"I hope that's food," called Dugan.

"Not unless you want salad," replied Emmett.

"The world's tiniest salad," laughed Bryndis.

The trays were filled with seedlings arranged in neat rows. Each green sprout was tucked into its own little square pocket of potting soil.

"The botanical nursery sent up these starts for us to plant," said Emmett. "Bryndis has *Impatiens gordonii* and I've got *Nepenthes pervillei*."

"Dr. Chavreau says these varieties are found only in Seychelles," said Bryndis. "The impatiens were once thought to be extinct until someone found one growing on one of the islands. My impatiens go in the shade, but Emmett's pitcher plants need sunlight."

Pitcher plants? Cruz peered into Emmett's tray at the clusters of tiny, narrow green leaves that formed a star shape. The test-tube-shaped pitcher blossoms were just beginning to develop.

Sailor was leaning in, too. "They're carnivorous, right?"

"Yep," said Emmett. "The bright yellow pitcher blossom attracts insects. The bugs come to drink nectar from around the rim, lose their footing on the slippery edge, and fall into the pitcher to be digested as dinner. The cool part is *this* plant has some of the same acids as *our* stomachs."

"That *is* cool!" exclaimed Lani.

"When do *we* eat?" asked Dugan.

"Professor Gabriel is getting lunch ready," said Bryndis. "When we left, Dr. Chavreau and his team were starting back down the mountain. They're hauling out some of the branches from the bigger trees. Professor Gabriel said we'll eat, then hike down."

Emmett lifted his tray. "Once we plant these."

Sailor unscrewed the top from her water bottle. "You mean we're almost done?"

"Uh-huh."

"What are we waiting for?" Dugan rubbed the palms of his gloves together. "Bryndis, Lani and I can come with you, and Cruz and Sailor can go with Emmett. I ... I mean if that's okay with everyone."

It was. They agreed to meet back at the same spot in 20 minutes. Everyone grabbed their gear and packs, and the groups went their separate ways.

"We're supposed to look for a flag," said Emmett as the trio headed across the slope toward a clearing near the cliffs. "Dr. Chavreau told me he stuck one in the rocks above where he wants us to plant the seedlings. He said to put them in a foot or two apart, in the sun—"

"There it is." Sailor was pointing.

A small white flag attached to a twig was poking up between the rocks near the edge of the cliff. The paper triangle fluttered in the wind, which was beginning to pick up. Cruz lifted his face; the sea breeze felt good against his sticky skin.

They knelt in the dirt near the rocks. Sailor and Emmett began digging a series of small holes. Cruz noticed that the plant tray was actually two trays: a top tray with plants in their individual cups that fit inside a larger tray. He lifted out the upper section so he could push out each seedling from the bottom of its holder. There were 40 pitcher plants in all. Cruz had to be careful popping them out. They were so tiny and the packed dirt fell easily away from the roots. Soon, the three explorers got into an easy rhythm. Cruz would hand one stem to Sailor, then one to Emmett, then back to Sailor again.

Emmett took his plants without looking up or saying a word. His emoto-glasses were hidden behind the GPS sunglasses Fanchon had made to fit over the frames, so Cruz couldn't gauge what his friend was feeling. Funny, how much Cruz had come to depend on those glasses. He hoped Emmett never went back to normal ones.

Cruz had to know what his friend was thinking. "Emmett, I should have listened to you and Dugan when you said to go into the CAVE. If I had, we'd be working with the turtles right now, instead of doing this. I don't blame you for being mad at me. I'm sorry."

"Nothing to be sorry for." Emmett seemed genuinely surprised at Cruz's apology. "And I'm not mad, Cruz. The EggsTend was a *team* project. Kat's deploying it, and getting it out there is what's important, not who does it. Honestly, I'm kind of glad we got Habitat Help."

"You are?" gulped Cruz.

"You are?" echoed Sailor.

Emmett took off his sunglasses to wipe his forehead. His emoto-glasses were the color of ripe pears and tinged pink at the corners: the colors of contentment and truth. "Sure, pulling out plants is hard, but putting these guys in is fun. Although, it does make me kind of home-sick. If I was in Toronto now, my grandpa and I would be deciding what to plant this year."

Cruz had never heard Emmett talk about a garden before. "What do you grow?"

"Veggies, mostly. Beans, snow peas, lettuce ..."

Cruz was a bit disappointed. He half expected Emmett to tell him about some strange plants—maybe even one he'd created, like a talking daisy or a venomous tulip.

Emmett was still listing stuff. "... cukes, tomatoes, pumpkins—"

"Pumpkins?" That got Sailor's attention. "We grow pumpkins, too."

"Have you ever heard of Baby Boos?" asked Emmett. She shook her head. "They're miniature white pumpkins. The rinds are soft. Slugs and snails like to munch holes in them, so to protect them, we train the vines to grow up the trellis next to our shed. Then at harvest time, we climb onto the roof and pick them."

"They sound great! I'll ask my mom to see if she can find the seeds."

"My grandpa can send some," offered Emmett. "We've got plenty."

"Thanks," said Sailor. "Hey, do you think Chef Kristos would let us plant a few Baby Boos in *Orion's* greenhouse?"

"Let's ask when we get back."

"We could train the vine to go up to the top of the observatory!"

"Could be tricky harvesting them," reminded Emmett.

"I'll do it," Sailor said bravely.

"I can see it now," said Emmett. "You climb to the top of the Baby Boo stalk and find a goose that lays golden eggs."

"And a giant," giggled Sailor.

Cruz's head bounced between his friends. What was this? He was used to refereeing their squabbling matches, not watching them joke and laugh. Cruz wondered, was there some kind of . . . thing happening between Sailor and Emmett?

Emmett had his hand out, waiting for a plant. Cruz pushed the seedling from its pocket and carefully set it in his friend's palm. Emmett slid the plant into a hole and, steadying the wire-thin stem between his thumb and index finger, scooped dirt around its leaves. He patted the dirt down as if wishing the little sprout good luck.

Once the last start had been planted, they poured water from their bottles over all 40 pitcher plants.

"It would be cool to come back and check on them," said Emmett. "You know, in a year or two . . ."

"I'm in," said Cruz.

Sailor smiled. "Me too."

It was a deal. They would come back to check on their pitcher plants. One day.

"It's almost time to meet up," said Emmett.

"I'll get the flag," said Sailor, getting to her feet. She began carefully picking her way through the sharp black rocks.

While Emmett shook the dirt from the spades, Cruz placed the smaller, now empty, tray inside the larger one.

"Cruz! Sailor! Emmett!"

Dugan was running through the brush toward them. Bryndis and Lani were right on his heels.

"We got done early . . ." panted Dugan, a backpack falling from each shoulder. "... so we thought we'd go ... help Professor Gabriel with lunch but ... when we got there ..."

"He was gone," huffed Lani.

"We found his backpack on a log," gasped Bryndis. "He had the food cooler out, like he'd started getting lunch ready, but ..."

"Maybe Dr. Chavreau's team had an emergency," said Emmett.

"Maybe," said Dugan. "But then why didn't Professor Gabriel tell us he was leaving?"

He was right. Professor Gabriel would never have left without saying something to at least one of them.

Cruz slapped his comm pin.

"It won't work," clipped Lani before he could open his mouth. "We tried. We got no response from anyone—not Professor Gabriel, not other teams, not even Taryn."

"Our phones and tablets are down, too," added Bryndis. "There's no online access."

Cruz felt his heart skip. "We're completely cut off?"

Three heads rapidly nodded.

"Guys!" The white flag in her hand, Sailor was hopping across the rocks as if they were hot coals. "I was looking out ... the bay ... the ship ..." She stumbled and the flag fell from her fingers. Cruz caught her by the shoulders and, as he righted her, Sailor's terrified eyes met his. "*Orion* is ... gone!"

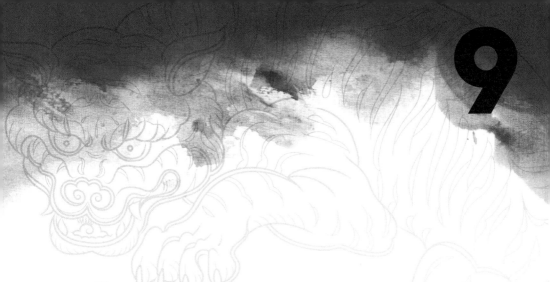

▶ **"ÓTRÚLEGT!"** said Bryndis. She saw their puzzled stares. "Uh ... I mean ... unbelievable!"

"I saw this in a movie once," said Dugan. "Tourists on an island started disappearing, one by one."

"Relax. Nobody is after *us*," said Sailor, but she shot Cruz a private look that asked, *Are they?*

Nebula wouldn't try something out here, would they? They had proved they were capable of anything, anywhere, so it *was* possible ...

"In the movie, the villains were aliens," Dugan was still chattering. "Hungry ones. And they weren't in the mood for burgers and fries, if you know what I mean."

"Sure, it could be brain-sucking aliens, or"—Emmett gave Dugan a grin—"Captain Iskandar might have moved the ship to solve the communications problem."

"That makes sense," sighed Bryndis. "The second one, I mean."

"It still doesn't explain what happened to Professor Gabriel," said Lani.

"No comms. No professor. And now no ship." Dugan groaned. "Could this day get *any* worse?"

Cruz felt something cold on his head. He glanced up into a dark gray sky. A drop of water tapped his forehead. Another splashed onto his cheek.

"I think it just did," muttered Sailor.

In a matter of seconds, the droplets became a downpour. The race was on to unzip their collars and pop up their rain hoods. Was that a flash of lightning?

Cruz waved to his teammates. "We need to find—"

Boom! A peal of thunder rattled his teeth.

"That way!" Emmett was motioning to a rocky outcrop about 10 yards up the trail.

As everyone ran for cover, Cruz slung Professor Gabriel's pack over his free shoulder. Loaded down with food and supplies, it was several pounds heavier than his own pack. Juggling both bags, Cruz was the last one under the ledge and more than a little out of breath.

Team Cousteau huddled under the overhang, watching the rain fall sideways in sheets. Water cascaded off the tips of the palm leaves like miniature waterfalls. It wasn't long before two small rivers formed on either side of the main trail. The explorers stood in awe, watching the swift and powerful current carry twigs, leaves, and other debris down the hill.

"It's like something out of one of Monsieur Legrand's training lessons," said Sailor.

"Except we can't end this program," said Lani.

"I hope Professor Gabriel has found shelter, too," Bryndis said softly. "Wherever he is."

"We should start a search," said Dugan.

"Not a good idea in a thunderstorm," cautioned Emmett. "We'll have to sit tight."

"*We* might have to wait, but"—Cruz opened his jacket pocket—"Mell, on. Come to eye level, please."

His honeybee drone obeyed.

"A search bee!" cried Bryndis.

"Mell, we need for you to locate Professor Gabriel," instructed Cruz. "Access your memory for his photo, then do a sweep within a three-quarter-mile radius of this position. If you find him, take a video recording, note his location, and return immediately."

"Three-quarters of a mile?" questioned Dugan.

"That's her communication range using the pin remote," explained Sailor. "If she goes beyond that, he'll lose contact."

Cruz turned to the little MAV hovering next to him. "Mell, ready?"

Golden eyes blinked.

"Remember, three-quarters of a mile—no farther," he whispered. "And be careful."

She cocked her head as if to say, *Aren't I always?*

He managed a grin. "Mell, go."

Bzzzz! Helicoptering up, the MAV made a tight turn and zipped away.

"Good one." Bryndis bent toward him. "You said *be* careful to your bee."

"I did?" Cruz hadn't meant to make the pun.

Her smile slowly faded. "It's really coming down. Will she be okay?"

"Mell's watertight," Cruz assured her. "She can even float, if she has to. If the rain gets too much for her, though, she'll come back."

The weather wasn't worrying Cruz, but something else was. Out here, a bird or bat could mistake Mell for a real insect. A predator might not swallow her, but it could certainly do plenty of damage—enough so that she wouldn't be able to communicate with him or be able to return. Without online access, Cruz would have no way to locate her. Mell would be lost. Forever.

Emmett began handing out food from Professor Gabriel's pack. Cruz took a turkey, Swiss, and tomato sandwich on whole wheat. The pack also contained grapes, protein bars, and Chef Kristos's homemade brownies, but Cruz turned them all down. He never could eat when he was nervous. He managed to choke down half his sandwich, then wrapped up the rest.

Restless, Cruz began to pace. Sailor was leaning out of the shelter, holding her water bottle under one of the leaf waterfalls. Cruz shuffled past Emmett, who was licking chocolate off his fingers, toward Lani. She was kneeling next to their teacher's open backpack.

Cruz watched her paw through it. "If you're looking for a brownie, I think Emmett is polishing off the last one."

"Nah. I was looking for clues but everything seems normal. All of Professor Gabriel's gear is here: MC camera, first aid kit, computer tablet, sunscreen, water purification tablets..." Lani glanced up, absently watching the rainwater fill Sailor's bottle. Seconds later, Lani was spinning Professor Gabriel's backpack. "It's gone!" she gasped.

"What is?" asked Cruz.

"His water bottle. Do you think he figured he could make it to a stream or river and get back before we finished planting our seedlings?"

Cruz nodded. "And he got lost."

"Or hurt," said Lani. She put a hand to her uniform. "If only our comm pins were working."

"If only *something* was working!" Sailor screwed the top back on her water bottle.

"It is." Dugan popped a grape into his mouth. "Our GPS should be okay."

"He's right!" Emmett sat up. "Our pins are linked to Earth's space satellites. They don't rely on ground signals or *Orion*."

Cruz turned to the rock wall and pressed the globe pin attached to his uniform. "Show me a map of Morne Seychellois National Park."

Moments later, a holographic map of the mountain appeared, with a blue dot identifying their current position.

"If *our* GPS pins are functioning, it's likely that Professor Gabriel's is, too," concluded Emmett.

If their teacher wasn't lost, that left only one other possibility: injury.

Cruz hit his GPS pin. "Show freshwater sources within a one-mile radius."

A moment later, the little globe projected two red dots onto a holo-map—one about half a mile to the southeast and another two miles to the north. All eyes zeroed in on the closest dot.

"It's within Mell's search area," said Cruz. "If he's there, she'll find him."

Bryndis studied the map. "Now that we know where he probably is, should we wait for Mell or go?"

Cruz had never sent Mell on a mission quite like this before. He had no idea how long it would take the MAV to locate Professor Gabriel. She could be back in a few minutes or a few hours.

"The rain is letting up." Lani got to her feet. "I say we go."

Cruz agreed. He glanced at Dugan, who usually had a reason why Team Cousteau couldn't or shouldn't do something. With a smirk, Dugan tipped his head toward Lani. "What she said."

Everyone went for their gear. Emmett took Professor Gabriel's pack. Cruz knew it was a little lighter now that they'd eaten, but it was still heavier than any of those the explorers carried.

"We'll take turns with the professor's pack," Cruz said to his roommate. "Let me know when you want me to take over."

"Okay. Thanks."

Putting up his hood, Cruz gazed out into the rain. He hated leaving without Mell.

"She'll be okay." Lani read his thoughts. She touched the honeycomb remote on Cruz's chest. "As long as you're wearing this, she'll come back."

If she hasn't run into trouble, he thought.

The sooner Mell returned, the better.

The downpour may have eased, but the rain had turned the path into a giant mudslide. With Cruz and his GPS map leading the way, Team Cousteau trudged through the gloppy mess in single file. Cruz headed south for about a quarter mile, then took the southeast fork, as directed by his GPS. It branched off onto a path that was much worse than the one they had come down—thinner, steeper, and much more overgrown. Cruz had to chop through branches with every step. He was glad his legs and arms were protected by his uniform, or he would have been covered in scratches. Every so often, Cruz tried contacting Professor Gabriel and *Orion* but got no response. The rain turned to drizzle, then petered out. Cruz pushed back his hood. Taking a sharp turn, he heard a rumbling sound. He looked up. More thunder?

Suddenly, Cruz was sliding!

He tried to pedal backward but couldn't get traction in the mud. He threw out both arms, hands grabbing, fingers reaching. Wet ferns slipped through his palms. There was nothing to hold on to. Cruz was falling...

His right shoulder was on fire, but he was no longer being thrust forward. Someone had clamped a hand around his upper arm. Cruz kicked like mad to get his feet under him. When, finally, he felt ground beneath his heels, Cruz saw that he was teetering on the edge of a crumbling drop-off. The trail and everything ahead of it was gone! All that was in front of him was a fatal plunge to a river several hundred feet below. On the opposite hill, a waterfall surged over a sheer black granite cliff.

Sailor had a firm grip on his right arm. "What is it with you and waterfalls anyway?" she shouted above the roaring water.

Bzzz! Bzzz!

"Mell!" Cruz was so excited to see her, he lost his footing again. Everything began to swirl—the trees, the cliff, the waterfall, his stomach. He felt another hand. His heart was beating faster than a hummingbird's, and he could barely breathe as he looked up into the eyes of his rescuer. "Thanks, Lani," he rasped.

The girls hauled Cruz in, and the team backtracked to a safe distance.

Bzzzzz! Mell flashed her eyes two times, paused, then flashed them twice again.

"She's got ... something," huffed Cruz, his heart still wildly pounding. "A holo-video ... Mell, play."

Within seconds, the explorers were gasping in horror! Soaked and covered in mud, Professor Gabriel was clinging to a boulder with one arm; the other arm was crushed awkwardly against his chest. The slope appeared to be hollowed out, the soil loose. Below the video, Mell projected the same GPS trail map Team Cousteau had been following. Professor Gabriel's location was marked with a yellow star. Cruz moved to layer his GPS map over Mell's. The red dot overlapped the southern point of the star.

They had done it. They had found Professor Gabriel! Reaching him, however, was another matter. If the maps were accurate, their instructor was somewhere below the drop-off that had nearly dumped Cruz hundreds of feet into the gorge.

"He must have been heading to the river for water and gotten caught in the landslide that took out the trail," surmised Dugan.

"He's holding his arm close, like he's hurt," said Emmett.

Sailor nodded. "We need to pinpoint his exact location."

"*And* hope we can get to it," said Cruz. "Mell, can you get us to a safe spot above Professor Gabriel?"

Flashing her eyes, the bee turned and flew west along the edge of the hillside. She stayed at shoulder level and traveled slowly so they could keep up. This section of the slope was rockier and seemed a bit more stable to Cruz than where they had come from. At least, he hoped so. Mell was going out beyond the edge of the hill. Hovering, she turned to face the explorers and blinked her eyes.

"He's here," interpreted Cruz. "Mell, how far down is Professor Gabriel?"

A moment later, she projected the answer onto his chest. Seeing the faces of his teammates, Cruz didn't need to read the upside-down numbers to know the news wasn't good. But he did anyway: *141.4 feet.*

It was too far down to reach without climbing gear. They had no ropes, no crampons, no helmets—nothing.

"Everybody, see if you have anything we can use to rappel," said Cruz. He unzipped his own pack, though he knew it didn't contain anything that would help. Lani caught his eye and shook her head. The others were doing the same.

"What about one of these bloody things?" Sailor was tugging on a thick creeping vine.

"Not long enough," said Emmett. "Or strong enough."

"Maybe we could tie our clothes together," suggested Bryndis.

"I doubt we're wearing one hundred forty-one point four feet of clothes," said Dugan. "Unless you've got twenty layers of underwear on."

He was right. That plan wasn't going to work.

Tip, tap. Tip, tap.

It was starting to rain again.

Standing beside Cruz, Bryndis laced her fingers through his. He squeezed her hand. She squeezed back.

Wet, and getting wetter by the second, the members of Team Cousteau could only stare at one another. Nobody had any ideas on how to save Professor Gabriel.

And they were running out of time.

10

▶ **"IF WE WERE BACK** on *Orion,*
Monsieur Legrand would help us," said Bryndis, flipping up her hood.

"If we were back on *Orion,* Monsieur would have parachuted in by now to point out everything we'd done wrong and make us start all over again," drawled Dugan.

Cruz smiled at the image of their survival instructor gliding in from above to save the—

Of course!

Releasing Bryndis's hand, Cruz took several steps away from their circle. He reached around to the back of his collar, searching, his thumb glossing over the letter *P.* He latched on to the tab, giving it a hard tug. The top lining of his jacket gave way, jettisoning yards of gold and black silk out behind him.

"Our parachutes!" Sailor threw up her arms.

"Brilliant." Turning from blue to pink to yellow, Emmett's glasses looked like a basket of pastel-colored Easter eggs. "I'd say we've probably got about thirty feet of chute and lines each."

That's what Cruz was betting, too. If he was right, that should be more than enough to reach Professor Gabriel. However, if he was wrong . . .

Everyone began releasing their chutes, too. Cruz wrestled out of his jacket, then popped open the metal clips that attached the suspension lines to his uniform. The explorers wasted no time stretching out their chutes along the trail and attaching them, end to end. Cruz knotted his suspension cords to Sailor's top pilot chute, which was located above her main chute. She then tied her suspension cords to Lani's pilot chute, who attached her cords to Dugan's chute, and so on until they had a complete chain of chutes and lines. Mell measured their parachute rope at 166.3 feet. It was more than enough!

"All set." Emmett hopscotched through the lines. "One of us is going to need to rappel to get the rope on Professor Gabriel—"

"I'll do it," declared Cruz and Dugan in unison.

"It should be me." Dugan puffed out his chest and shot Cruz a defiant look. "First, I've been climbing longer than you. Second, I'm the strongest one on the team. And third...uh...uh...I called it before you did."

Seriously? That was his argument? Cruz felt his temper start to bubble. He had beaten Dugan in the Augmented Reality Challenge back at Rock Creek Park, which had included a difficult rock climb. "First, you may have been climbing longer than me but that doesn't mean you're better," he countered. "Second, I'd put my money on Sailor in an arm wrestling contest with you any day. And third, sorry, but you didn't call dibs before me. We tied."

Dugan's mouth formed a tight line. He narrowed his eyes at Cruz, who glared right back. They stared each other down, daring the other to blink first.

"Let's not argue," said Bryndis.

"Who's arguing?" growled Dugan.

"Not me," clipped Cruz, his eyes getting drier by the second.

"I...uh...I think I should go," said a quiet yet determined voice.

Cruz broke off the staring contest to look at his best friend. Lani had her hand up near her chin and was wiggling her fingers. "It makes the most sense. Dugan, you *are* strong, which is exactly why we need you here to help pull up Professor Gabriel. Since I'm probably the lightest, it'll be easiest to bring me up. Plus, over the break, Monsieur

Legrand had me do the same ARC that you guys did back in D.C. and . . . well, I beat both your times." Her gaze settled on Cruz. "Yours by fourteen seconds."

Cruz swallowed hard. "You did? Why didn't you tell me?"

"Never came up."

Cruz knew she was a good climber, but he hadn't realized she was *that* good.

"Uh . . . guys?" Emmett leaned in. "We're wasting time. I think Lani's right."

"Yep," said Sailor. "I vote Lani."

"Lani," said Bryndis, giving Cruz an apologetic look.

It was already four votes to two. Cruz wasn't going to win this one. "Okay," he surrendered, though he wasn't thrilled about giving in. He still thought it should have been him.

Dugan stuck a toe in the muck but mumbled "Fine."

"Thanks, Dugan." Lani patted his arm, which seemed to cheer him up. A little.

Cruz and Sailor attached the suspension lines of the last chute in the makeshift rope to Lani's jacket. Cruz tugged on the clips to make sure they were secure, then held out the coat for Lani to slip her arms into. She zipped up her jacket. Dugan and Bryndis hurried to wrap the other end of the chute rope to the trunk of a sturdy palm tree about 15 feet from the edge of the cliff. Team Cousteau spread themselves out along the rope a few feet apart—Emmett nearest the tree, then Sailor, Bryndis, Dugan, and Cruz, who was closest to the edge of the hill. Team Cousteau looked like they were about to play tug-of-war, but they all knew this was no game.

Grabbing the lines of the makeshift rope attached to her jacket, Lani pulled down on them, wrapping them around her waist several times. Cruz saw that her hands were trembling. Her face was pale and the front of her damp hair clung to her forehead, making her look younger than her 12 years.

Lani's eyes were searching his. "Don't you think I can do it?"

It wasn't that he didn't have confidence in her. Cruz knew that when Leilani Kealoha set her mind to something, she usually accomplished it. But this . . . this was dangerous. The hillside was already saturated and more rain was falling. At any moment, another chunk of the unstable slope could break off, taking Lani and Professor Gabriel with it. "I *know* you can do it," Cruz said with more confidence than he felt. "Mell, take Lani to Professor Gabriel. Stay with her. Wait for her instructions."

Two large golden eyes blinked in confirmation.

"It won't take Mell long to get back to me," Cruz said to Lani, "so make sure Professor Gabriel is ready before you send her up."

"I will."

"Be sure to use Mell's name *before* every command. She gets confused if you don't—"

"I will. Cruz, I know how she works. I programmed her remote, remember?"

"Right." Cruz picked up the rope. The silk felt cool and slick in his fingers. He wound it loosely around his wrists. "We'll give you slack as you need it. Take your time going down. But don't go too slowly. And don't go too fast."

She gave him an annoyed look.

"Sorry."

Lani placed her left hand above her right on the rope, turned to face Cruz, and scooted back until her heels teetered off the ledge. She leaned back, testing to see if the rope would hold her weight. It did.

"I'll be here," said Cruz, his breath catching in his throat.

"I know. That's what I'm counting on." Lani clamped down on the rope. "See ya, *hoaaloha*."

And she was gone.

Inch by inch, foot by foot, the chute rope slid through Cruz's hands and over the hill. Cruz did his best to guide it and keep the lines from tangling or getting caught on brush. Behind him, he could hear his teammates doing the same thing.

"Emmett, it's snagged on that stump!" yelled Sailor.

"I see it … I see it!"

"Twisted line!" shouted Dugan.

"Got it!" answered Bryndis.

As they let out more and more line, Cruz started to get more and more worried. What if Lani couldn't reach Professor Gabriel? What if their teacher was severely injured? What if the five of them couldn't pull him back up?

The rope. It had stopped!

Cruz kept his gaze fixed on the exact spot where Lani had gone over. He held his breath, his eyes scanning the horizon for Mell. As the minutes ticked by, Cruz began to get panicky. What was taking so long?

Finally, after nine agonizing minutes …

Bzzz!

"Mell's here!" Cruz called back to the others.

The MAV flew straight for Cruz, coming in for a landing on his forearm. Mell projected an image of Lani in the air, then began to play the video she'd recorded.

"I've reached … Professor Gabriel." Lani was breathing hard. "He's conscious, but he's hurt his shoulder … I think it might be dislocated. His legs are fine, though I can tell he's pretty tired. I've given him some water and a protein bar." Her face loomed close, Mell's fish-eye lens making Lani's eyes look enormous. "Go slowly, okay? I think he might be injured worse than he's letting on." She glanced away, up the hill, as if she'd heard something. Lani's brow wrinkled but Cruz couldn't see what she was looking at. "Mell, stop recording."

Cruz exhaled. It was now up to them. Team Cousteau had to get Professor Gabriel and Lani up safely.

"She's ready!" Cruz hollered over his shoulder. He gave his teammates a few minutes to get set. Then, digging his heels into the soggy ground, Cruz hauled two giant handfuls of silk toward him. He extended his arms and repeated the move. It was sort of like rowing a boat.

Reach forward. Grab. Pull back.

Reach forward. Grab. Pull back.

On and on, he went. His arms started to cramp, but Cruz did not slow down. Once, his foot slipped and he fell flat on his back but he didn't let go of the rope—he merely got his feet back under him and continued rowing. Cruz towed in silk and suspension lines for what seemed like forever. Then he saw it—a hand!

Five dirty fingers were clawing ... reaching ... grabbing ...

"He's here!" screamed Cruz, setting himself. "We've got him!"

He saw Sailor and Emmett whiz past. While they helped Professor Gabriel over the ledge, Cruz, Bryndis, and Dugan held the rope steady. Once their professor was up on solid ground, everyone collapsed. It took several minutes for the fire in Cruz's shoulders to stop burning.

"Thanks ... I'm all right," panted Professor Gabriel. "But ... Lani ... the hill isn't stable ... need to hurry ..." He tried to sit up. "Arrrrgh!"

"I'll get the first aid kit," said Sailor. She shot Cruz a look that said, *I'll handle this. You rescue Lani.*

"Let's get Lani up *now*," Cruz barked to his teammates. He tied a small log onto the end of the rope and threw it over the side. Dugan, Emmett, and Bryndis started flinging the rest of the rope over as well.

"Mell, start recording." Cruz stared into a pair of gold eyes. "Lani, we have Professor Gabriel, and we're sending the rope back down for you now. The professor says the slope could go at any time, so let's make this quick. Send Mell up when you're ready for us to pull. Mell, stop recording. Find Lani. Mell, *go!*"

Cruz ran to help his team throw out more rope. His arms still ached from pulling up Professor Gabriel, but he wasn't about to stop. To be safe, they let out several more feet of line than they had used to bring up their teacher. Everyone took up their positions along the rope once again and waited for Mell's return. Sailor joined them after she'd gotten a sling on Professor Gabriel's arm and propped him up against a tree trunk.

Three minutes passed ... then six ... then nine ...

Ten minutes! One minute longer than last time.

"The rope could be caught on something," shouted Dugan.

Cruz feared it was far worse than that. He'd instructed Mell to find Lani. The only reason she wouldn't be able to complete the task was if...

Lani wasn't there.

No. Cruz refused to let himself even consider the possibility. Another minute. They'd give her another minute.

"Taryn Secliff to Professor Gabriel."

"Yes, yes, I'm here!" said their instructor. "Taryn, I hear you."

"Thank goodness. We've been trying to reach you for hours. We had a communications issue on board, along with a power outage—talk about a nightmare of a day."

"I know the feeling."

"Is everyone on your team all right?"

"I've had an accident," said Professor Gabriel. "I'm hurt, but I can hike out. We're waiting for one more team member to return, then we'll head down the mountain..."

Cruz checked his OS band. Fourteen minutes! Mell should have been back by now.

He'd waited long enough. Cruz began hauling in rope as fast as he could. "I'm going after her!"

"Cruz, you can't," said Dugan.

"Oh no?" shrieked Cruz, going even faster. He was not about to hear any of Dugan's dumb excuses. "Because we haven't given her enough time? Because she could be buried by now? Because you called it first? I don't care about any of that—"

"No." Dugan was beside him, a hand on his shoulder. "Because she's coming this way."

Cruz's head popped up. Lani was heading through the brush along the edge of the hill. Her face was streaked with mud. Rain plastered her hair to her head. Still, she was swinging her arms, marching with purpose. As she closed the distance between them, Cruz saw that Mell was with her. The drone floated protectively above her left shoulder.

Cruz let go of the rope. And ran. He ran faster than he'd ever run before.

"I know, I know!" cried Lani when she caught sight of him. "I was supposed to wait for the rope, but that part of the hill was starting to go ... I found a few footholds that got me to the granite ..."

Cruz threw his arms around her so hard, he heard the air leave her lungs.

Still, Lani kept talking, but he wasn't listening. Her words, their teammates, even the rain—Cruz heard none of it. The voice in his head drowned out everything.

She's all right.

She's all right.

She's all right.

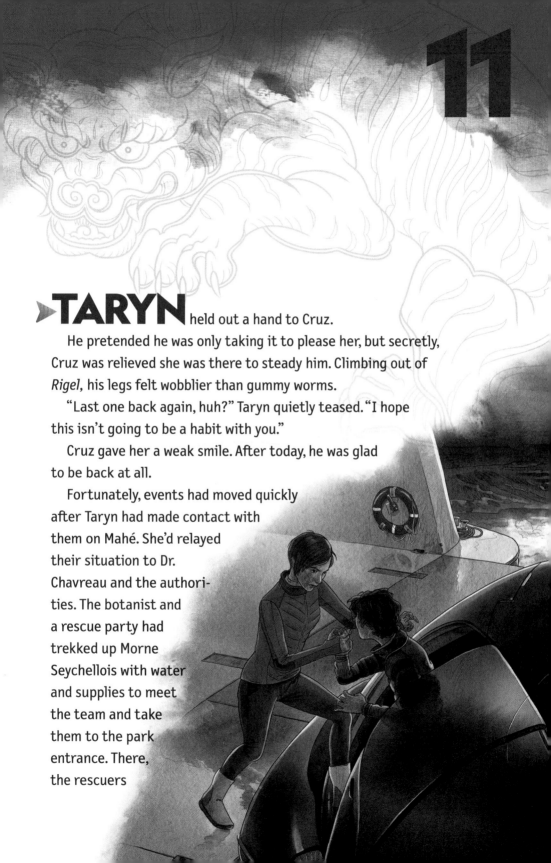

11

▶TARYN held out a hand to Cruz.

He pretended he was only taking it to please her, but secretly, Cruz was relieved she was there to steady him. Climbing out of *Rigel,* his legs felt wobblier than gummy worms.

"Last one back again, huh?" Taryn quietly teased. "I hope this isn't going to be a habit with you."

Cruz gave her a weak smile. After today, he was glad to be back at all.

Fortunately, events had moved quickly after Taryn had made contact with them on Mahé. She'd relayed their situation to Dr. Chavreau and the authorities. The botanist and a rescue party had trekked up Morne Seychellois with water and supplies to meet the team and take them to the park entrance. There, the rescuers

transported Professor Gabriel to the hospital in Victoria, while
Dr. Chavreau escorted Team Cousteau to the pier to meet Jaz.

Emmett's deduction that Captain Iskandar had moved the ship to
help with their communications issue had proved correct. *Orion* was
now anchored on the other side of Mahé. It had taken Team Cousteau
close to a half hour to return via hovercraft.

As the explorers stood on the lower aft deck, Taryn handed them
towels. "Power's back up for most of the ship, but it's still touch-and-go,
so don't be surprised if you lose your lights a few times tonight."

"Sound like we weren't the only ones who had a rough day," said
Emmett.

"When it rains, it pours," said their adviser.

"Please, Taryn." Sailor buried her face in her towel. "Let's never say
the R-word again."

Taryn laughed.

"How's Professor Gabriel?" asked Cruz.

"Stable," she answered. "They're keeping him overnight for x-rays
and tests." She surveyed them. "How about you guys? Anything need
tending? Cuts, bruises, bug bites, sunburns, allergic reactions, sprained
ankles, sprained anything?"

They shook their heads.

"It's a miracle." She sighed. "If you're all toweled off, you can head on
up to your cabins. Take your tablets and gear but leave your packs and
jackets. I'll see to it that everything is cleaned and that your jackets
get new chutes. You can wear your lightweight jackets for the time
being. After you get cleaned up, go get dinner."

Sailor yawned. "I'm really tired. Can't we go to—"

"It's not a request," said Taryn. "Eat first. Then sleep. You'll have to
be content with whatever Chef Kristos was able to whip up within the
last hour—probably soup and sandwiches."

"Sounds perfect," said Lani.

Emmett nudged Cruz. "I wonder if it's tomato soup and grilled
cheese."

The reference to his first meal in Washington, D.C., made Cruz chuckle. That day at the airport when he'd met Emmett and Sailor seemed like ages ago. "You know," Cruz said to his roommate, "we never did build that time machine we talked about."

"The year's not over yet," said Emmett. His emoto-glasses signaled he wasn't kidding.

Dugan led the way up the steps, followed by Sailor, Bryndis, Emmett, Cruz, and Lani.

"On second thought..." Taryn called. "Why don't you take off your socks and shoes here? I'll catch it from housekeeping if they spot muddy footprints leading to your cabins."

Cruz sank onto the right side of the bottom stair. Lani took the left side of the same step. Sitting next to her, Cruz couldn't hide his smile. She looked like she'd been playing tackle football. And lost. Her hair had dried, but without a brush to style it, a piece on the side was sticking up.

"What?" asked Lani. She'd caught him looking.

"I...uh...was thinking...dye your hair pink and you could be a dead ringer for a troll doll."

"Yeah?" She raised an eyebrow. "You're not exactly Prince Charming, you know, with that mud mustache."

Cruz quickly wiped his mouth on his towel.

Bryndis was perched four steps above him. When their eyes met, his smile widened. He waited for her to return the grin, but she glanced down instead. Her blond hair fell like a curtain over her face as she began prying off her boot. She had to be exhausted. He certainly was.

Taryn wove her way up the stairs between them. "Oh, I almost forgot." She paused at the landing.

Cruz stifled his groan. Dugan didn't. It couldn't be time for their room inspection again, could it? Emmett and Cruz's cabin wasn't a mess, but it certainly wasn't ready for their adviser's monthly walkthrough. Taryn's eagle eye didn't miss a thing.

"I do not say this lightly." Taryn's voice cracked. "I do not say it often.

In fact, it is unlikely you will ever hear it from me again."

Cruz froze, a boot in his hands. The rest of his team had become statues, too. Six explorers looked up at their adviser, now towering over them. Had they done something wrong? Were they in trouble?

Taryn laid her hands on her heart, one over the other, to make an X. She took a slow, deep breath. "I have never been prouder of an Explorer Academy team than I am of you today. Nicely done, Team Cousteau. Nicely done."

AN HOUR LATER, showered and in clean uniforms, Cruz, Sailor, Emmett, and Lani were striding down the faculty passage. They'd stopped for a quick bite: ham and cheese sandwiches and vegetable alphabet soup with Greek letters, naturally, because Chef Kristos was from Athens. The lights in the corridor flickered. It was 7:30, too early for Taryn's lights-out signal.

Lani lifted her eyes. "Stay on, power."

Cruz rapped on the door of cabin 241. "I hope the tech lab stays up." The thought of Fanchon's weird experiments not being properly heated, cooled, or caged made him shiver.

"The lab has its own auxiliary power source," replied Emmett.

The cabin door swung open.

"Thank goodness!" cried Sailor at the exact same time as Aunt Marisol.

Cruz's aunt stepped back, motioning them to come in. "Bryndis and Dugan, they're all right, too?"

"Everyone is okay," said Cruz, giving his aunt a quick hug. "But we still haven't heard about Professor Gabriel."

"It's only been a few hours." Releasing Cruz, Aunt Marisol shut the door behind them. "I'm sure Taryn will tell us as soon as she has news. I still can't believe it—a landslide! Professor Gabriel owes his life to you. It took some quick thinking to locate and rescue him."

"We're a good team." Sailor stifled a yawn. "A tired team, but a good one."

Aunt Marisol's forehead wrinkled. "You should all get some rest."

"We will," said Cruz, "but first we need to know..." He dipped his hand into his pocket and brought out the little Aztec crown charm. "Is this yours?"

For a moment his aunt stared at the charm as if it was cursed. She gently took it between her thumb and index finger. "It *is* mine. I never expected to see it again. I lost it... I don't even know how long ago. Where did you find it?"

"Mom had it," said Cruz. "It was in her box, the one you gave me from her office."

"It was?" Her frown deepened. "I don't remember seeing it, but that was a very difficult time. I suppose I didn't really go through everything thoroughly. I took the box, locked it up in my office at the Academy, and there it stayed until..."

"I came along," finished Cruz.

"I'm... confused." Aunt Marisol pushed her hair back. "I know I didn't give this charm to Petra. If she found it, why didn't she return it?"

Cruz shrugged. "I don't know. I'm not sure how she got it. I only know she needed it."

"Needed it? For what?"

"To help me find one of her cipher pieces. In her journal, she said you were her best friend, and she had a trinket from your life. She told me to remember that the *third* time was the charm. This morning, Lani noticed that the second charm on your bracelet was missing."

"See, I thought the crown might go in that spot," broke in Lani, "And the charm next to it—the *third* one—might lead us to the next piece of the cipher."

Aunt Marisol went to her mirrored jewelry box sitting on top of her dresser and opened the top drawer. She reached in, then came back to the coffee table in front of her sofa. Kneeling, she laid the charm bracelet flat on the table. The explorers gathered around. Every third link in the bracelet held a different charm. The first charm next to the clasp was a black-and-silver stepped Maya temple. The sixth link was empty. That must be where the Aztec crown went. Cruz's eyes rapidly found the ninth link. Attached to it was a white enamel, three-dimensional square building on a raised platform. The roof was made up of a teardrop-shaped dome surrounded by four smaller domes. Four towers stood on the platform, one opposite each corner of the building.

"The Taj Mahal," whispered Lani.

"That's right," said Aunt Marisol. "I used to buy handmade charms from the local artisans on my travels. I got this when I visited the tomb in my first year as a teacher with the Academy."

Remembering Lani's research, Cruz tapped one of the pillars with the edge of his fingernail. "These are minarets, aren't they?"

"That's right," said his aunt.

Cruz was beginning to understand. He could tell by his friends' expressions that they were, too.

Emmett pointed to each tower. "Southeast, southwest, northwest, and *northeast*."

The abbreviation for "northeast" was "NE."

NE MINARET.

The explorers were smiling. Aunt Marisol, however, was still playing catch-up. Cruz turned the crown charm over and showed her the engraving. "Have you ever seen this?"

She shook her head. "There was nothing on the back when I had it on my bracelet."

Good. It was fair to assume that the inscription was his mom's handiwork.

"At first, we read it as NEMINARET but that's probably because there wasn't enough room for a space between 'NE' and 'minaret' on the charm," explained Emmett. "We had no idea what a neminaret was."

"What's below it?" Aunt Marisol squinted. "Are those numbers?"

"1-1-2-9," said Cruz.

"Your birthday?" She drew back. "What does that mean?"

"We don't know," said Lani.

Sailor leaned on her elbows. "Not yet, anyway."

"The important thing is now we know where we have to go," said Cruz.

Yes, they knew.

All eyes were riveted to the miniature building dangling from Aunt Marisol's bracelet. They were going to the Taj Mahal. They were going to India.

12

AT THE SOUND of his alarm, Cruz's right hand automatically flung over his body to clamp on to his OS band. The alarm shut off. He rolled onto his stomach, then shoved his left hand under his pillow so that when his alarm went off again in five minutes, it would be muffled. Except the alarm didn't go off again. By the time Cruz opened his eyes, it was 13 minutes to eight. He bolted upright. "Emmett!"

"Huh?" groaned the lump opposite him.

"We overslept."

"Professor Gabriel ... hospital. Remember?"

"Do you honestly think Taryn is going to let us off the hook for first period? She'll probably teach it herself. Come on!"

Emmett kicked off his covers.

They had to skip showers and breakfast, but the boys made it to conservation with a minute to spare. Skidding into Manatee classroom, Cruz and Emmett noticed they weren't the only ones who could have used more sleep. People were melting into their desks. Heads were down. Voices flat. Yesterday's projects had clearly taken their toll. A nasty sunburn had colored Weatherly's cheeks chili pepper red. Tao had a ginormous mosquito bite on her neck.

Collapsing into his seat between Emmett and Lani, Cruz rested his chin on his palm. Bryndis was at her desk in the row ahead of him. Bent over her tablet, her fingers were flying over her touch-screen keyboard. Cruz closed his eyes. Just for a minute. With Professor Gabriel gone, he wondered, who would be their teacher? Fanchon? Dr. Vanderwick? Maybe Aunt Marisol?

"You awake?" said a girl's voice in his right ear.

He yawned. "Barely."

"I've got an idea."

"I'm glad somebody does."

"I'm talking about how to catch the spy."

That got his eyes open. Cruz turned to Lani. "How?"

"Here's what we do." She leaned on his desk. "You know how when Laundry finds stuff we forget to take out of our pockets they send us messages to come claim it, right? So, one night we send a note to the explorers, pretending we're Laundry, and say we've found a little black *rock* with an unusual inscription on it. You quickly respond and say it's your good-luck stone, then they—I mean, we—answer back to tell you to come by and identify it in the morning. Of course, we make sure all the explorers see the messages going both ways. Then, after Laundry closes, we hide out there and wait for whoever comes to try to steal the stone."

Cruz was impressed. Lani had clearly thought this through, however, she had forgotten one important detail. "Laundry has a security door, you know."

She gave him a look. "Do you really think a *door* is going to stop Nebula from getting what they think is the cipher? They've already broken into your room, attacked you in the CAVE, tampered with your UCC helmet, poisoned your duffel bag—"

"Okay, okay." He got the point.

Lani frowned. "Now that I think about it, I'm not so sure the security around here is all that hot." She shook her head. "Anyway, we'd also activate our shadow badges to stay hidden in the laundry—"

"We don't get to jump out and yell *Aha*?"

"No! You *never* tell the double agent you're onto him. Or her. That's

97

how you keep the upper hand. Once we know who the spy is, we can feed 'em all kinds of bad information about where you're going and what you're doing. We can completely throw Nebula off your trail."

"Lani, that's so sneaky."

She gave him a smug grin. "You're welcome."

Glancing up, Cruz saw Bryndis was no longer bent over her tablet. She'd twisted slightly in her seat and was looking his way. When their eyes met, Bryndis dropped her gaze, then turned to face forward. Was she mad at him? He wondered. Upset about something else? It wasn't like her not to give him a quick grin before class. He leaned forward to talk to her but never got the chance.

"Good morning." Professor Modi walked briskly into the room.

"Good morning," responded the explorers.

"I'm sure you've all heard about Professor Gabriel's harrowing incident yesterday and Team Cousteau's brave rescue."

The class clapped. Everyone except Ali, Cruz noted.

"Happy to report your teacher is doing well and resting comfortably," continued the professor. "However, he will need shoulder surgery ..."

There was a chorus of moans.

"When will he be back?" asked Felipe.

"Don't know. For the time being, I'll be teaching this class." He surveyed them. "I have some details about your new mission, but before I get to that let's wrap up the old one. Your post-mission reports are due by the end of the week. Please take out your tablets and answer the first set of questions now, while things are still fresh in your minds. We'll then break into teams and you'll start work on your oral reports ..."

"What do you think?" Lani was back, whispering in his ear. "Wanna catch a spy?"

Cruz tilted his head. "Upper hand, huh?"

"Totally."

He liked the sound of that. If the spy trap worked, he could stay one step ahead of Nebula. And if it didn't, no harm done. It was worth a try. "I'm in."

"Great." She turned to start the assignment.

"What's great?" Emmett said in his other ear.

"Lani's idea." Cruz related her plan to Emmett.

"That *is* a great plan. Or as Sailor would say, sweet as. She'll love it, by the way."

"Sailor?" Cruz gulped. "We ... uh ... can't tell Sailor, Emmett. Not this time. Not until we officially rule her out as the spy."

"Okay, but I wouldn't want to be in your boots when she finds out you snagged him without her."

"She's gonna be mad, huh?"

"Mad?" Emmett snorted. "Try furious. And not just because you left her out. Wait till she hears *she* was a suspect."

"What should I do?"

"What else? Trust her."

"I want to but how can I be sure she isn't—"

"You can't. You can't be a hundred percent sure about anybody, Cruz. Haven't you figured that out yet?" The emoto-glasses signaled his annoyance by becoming peach half-moons.

"I only meant—"

"Gentlemen?" Professor Modi was gesturing for them to get to work.

With apologetic nods, they obeyed.

Emmett was right. Sailor York was a loyal friend. Cruz knew there was no way he could have come as far as he had in finding his mother's formula without her. The more Cruz thought about Sailor being the spy, the more ridiculous the whole thing sounded.

Would a spy jump into a virtual waterfall with you? Stick by you when you were unfairly expelled from school? Risk her life for you over and over again?

Nuh-uh. No way. No how. Right?

Emmett was poking him, his glasses a contented apple green again. "Include Sailor in the plan," he said quietly. "If nobody shows at the laundry, then she goes to the top of your list of suspects. But if someone *does* take the bait, then Sailor's in the clear."

Cruz nodded.

"The best part," said Emmett, "is she won't ever know you doubted her."

Cruz rarely disagreed with his roommate, but this time he was wrong. The best part was he wouldn't risk losing one of his closest friends.

WHEN THE TEAM GATHERED at their usual table for lunch, Cruz took a seat next to Bryndis. As they crunched into their tacos and talked about what their next mission might be, she seemed fine. Still, a crowded dining room was no place to ask if something was bothering her. His next chance came after classes that day. Once Professor Benedict dismissed them, Cruz figured he would catch up to Bryndis in the passage, but she sped out of class at top speed.

Going down one side of the grand staircase, he couldn't navigate through the explorers to reach her. Everyone suddenly slowed. They were shifting to the right. Cruz quickly saw why. Fanchon was coming up that side of the steps. He could see her zebra-print head scarf.

"Exactly the people I'm looking for," said Fanchon. "Weatherly, Felipe, Shristine, and Cruz, do you guys have a sec?"

Cruz saw Weatherly and Shristine on the stairs ahead. A quick glance over his shoulder told him Felipe was a few steps behind him. The four explorers stopped, letting the class flow by. Cruz watched Bryndis reach the atrium, then turn left into the explorers' passage. She disappeared.

Fanchon had her hands on her hips. "Who's up for helping to test Planet Pup?"

Their robotic dog pal!

"It's fixed?" cried Weatherly.

"Yep. Or should I say 'woof!'"

"I gotta see this," said Felipe.

"Same here," said Cruz. He'd make sure to talk to Bryndis later.

Shristine and Weatherly were nodding, too.

"I'll grab everything from the lab and meet you guys in Taryn's cabin in ten minutes." Fanchon ran up the stairs, while the four explorers ran down. Cruz rushed to drop off his stuff. He was the first one to Taryn's cabin.

Hubbard trotted over to Cruz carrying his favorite green rubber ball. He plopped it down at Cruz's feet.

"Subtle hint, huh, bud?" Taryn grinned.

Cruz tossed the ball down the corridor. Hubbard bounded after it, tail high.

Taryn put a hand on Cruz's arm. "Stay after the test, okay? We need to talk."

"Okay." He knew what she wanted to discuss. Aunt Marisol had contacted the president of the Academy to tell her Cruz's next clue had led him to the Taj Mahal. Dr. Hightower had then called Taryn to arrange it, as she had done when he'd traveled to Petra to locate the third piece of the cipher.

Fanchon was coming down the passage, holding Planet Pup and its remote. Dr. Vanderwick was with her. In one arm, the tech lab assistant cradled a computer tablet twice the size of the explorers' version.

"At the structural level, a dog's brain is like ours," explained Fanchon, once everyone was assembled in Taryn's cabin. "They have the same chemicals and hormones that humans do, even oxytocin, which is connected to feelings of affection and love. However, emotionally, a canine's brain is more along the lines of a toddler, so there are certain limitations we have to recognize."

"For a human, we'd use a headset for BCI, or brain-computer interface," continued Dr. Vanderwick. "But since we can't do that with Hubbard, we created this." Reaching into the pocket of her lab coat, she held up a tiny black square no bigger than a binder clip. "While it might look small, this device can tap into the entire brain, allowing

Hubbard to use mind-control technology in the same way that we do. It has an embedded acquisition algorithm to respond to his mental commands that gets faster and more accurate with time."

Fanchon saw their puzzled faces. "The bot learns!" she exclaimed.

"Ohhhh!" they cried.

First, Dr. Vanderwick attached the small unit to the Westie's collar, then she began tapping her tablet screen.

Cruz felt a nudge on his calf. Hubbard let out the teeniest of whimpers. He wanted to play. Going down on one knee, Cruz scratched the dog between his ears. "In a minute, Hub. Soon, you'll be able to play all you want anytime you want. Won't that be fun?"

Hubbard cocked an ear as if to say, *Perhaps.*

"We're good to proceed," announced Dr. Vanderwick.

Fanchon hit the power button on Planet Pup. Four explorers automatically took a full step back. Everybody laughed. They remembered what had happened the last time they tried this.

"It's syncing with Hubbard's brain." Dr. Vanderwick read the data on her tablet. A minute later, she gave Fanchon a thumbs-up.

Fanchon released the disk. It quietly hovered next to Hubbard, a few inches off the floor. It sounded much better than when they'd first tested it in the conference room.

"This is incredible," said Weatherly. "It's going to work. I can feel it!"

Cruz felt the same way. He could hardly wait for Hubbard to make his choice: ball, disk, or stick?

Everybody watched and waited. Several minutes later, they were still watching and waiting.

"He has full control," whispered Dr. Vanderwick. "The bot is functioning normally."

"Why doesn't he choose?" asked Felipe.

"Maybe he isn't in the mood to play right now," said Shristine.

That seemed unlikely to Cruz. Hubbard was always up for a good game of fetch.

"Wait!" hushed Cruz. "There he goes."

Hubbard was moving toward Planet Pup! This was it! He was ready to play.

"I think he's going to want the stick," said Weatherly.

"I say the disk," countered Shristine.

Cruz was betting on the ball.

Instead of reaching up toward Planet Pup, however, the Westie bent his neck toward the floor. He tapped his nose against his old green ball. They watched the orb roll to Cruz. It stopped within an inch of his knee.

Well, Cruz *was* right about the ball part. With a sigh, Cruz patted Hubbard's head. "Guess you want to play fetch the old-fashioned way, huh?" Cruz rolled the ball across the room and Hubbard scurried after it.

"I'll work with him," said Taryn, blushing. "All he needs is a little practice. Thanks, everyone, for your hard work on Planet Pup. It's a wonderful gift."

Cruz, Weatherly, Shristine, and Felipe exchanged smiles. Even though things hadn't worked out quite as they'd planned, they were all glad they'd tried. For Cruz, it was the best Funday so far.

Everyone began filing out of the cabin. Cruz stayed behind.

"Soooooo," sang his adviser, closing the door. "Got a call this morning from Dr. Hightower. She says she's sending you, Emmett, Sailor, and Lani on a short mission this weekend. Wouldn't tell me what it was for or where you were going, only that I needed to make sure you were on the helicopter pad by seven o'clock Saturday morning."

There was no sense pretending this news was surprising, as he'd tried to do last time. She'd see right through him again.

"Thanks, Taryn," said Cruz. "I'll tell the others."

"You'll call me Saturday night so I won't worry?"

"I will."

Green eyes crinkled. "That's all. You are free to go, my dearest Cruz."

Cruz, nearly halfway to the door, suddenly turned. Closing the gap between them, he threw his arms around his adviser. One day, Cruz would tell her everything she didn't ask. And everything he couldn't say. That was a promise.

For now, though, this would have to do.

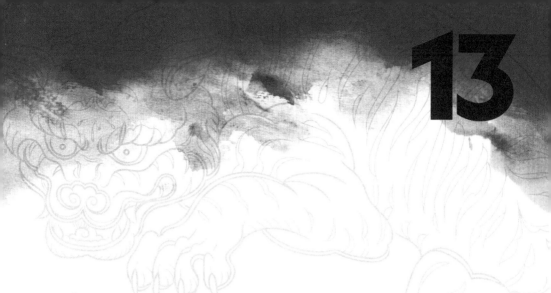

13

▶ **"NOBODY'S** coming," Sailor whispered from the darkness in front of Cruz.

"It hasn't even been twenty minutes," replied Lani, somewhere to Cruz's right. "It's like fishing. You've got to be patient."

"I hate fishing," said Sailor. "And my foot's asleep."

"I think Cruz is, too," chuckled Lani.

"I'm awake," said Cruz. He readjusted the towel covering his head, the only part of him besides his hands that his shadow badge hadn't camouflaged. They had considered borrowing Lumagine hoods and gloves from Fanchon, but they knew she would have asked too many questions. The towels would have to do.

"It's hot in here," said Sailor.

"It's the dryers," explained Lani. "Plus, we're right above the ship's engines."

"Will you guys keep it down?" shushed Emmett.

It was a good thing the ship's laundry room didn't have portholes. Emmett had activated his shadow badge along with the rest of them. But unlike Cruz, Lani, and Sailor, he did not blend in with the environment. He'd tried to mimic the explorers' yellow drawstring hamper bags stamped with a black *EA*. Unfortunately, Emmett looked more like a melting snowman with a spray-on tan. He'd wrapped his towel tight around his morphing frames so the only thing you could see were two small eyeholes.

Other than Emmett's fashion flub, everything else had gone off with-out a hitch. At precisely 6:45 p.m. (the laundry closed at seven), Lani had sent the fake message out to the explorers. Cruz had responded, and so on, as planned. Once the trap had been set, the four explorers had hightailed it down to Laundry on the main deck. They pressed their shadow badges outside the door and camouflaged their uniforms. They'd gotten lucky. Today was linens day, so the place was overflowing with sheets, blankets, and towels. Once A.J., the crewman at the counter, turned away, Cruz, Sailor, Lani, and Emmett darted between the laundry carts and the counter. In the back room, they dived into a heap of laundry next to the washing machines. Another crew member, who was taking clothes out of a dryer, didn't so much as look up. Minutes later, the staff finished work for the day and filed out, the security door latching firmly behind them.

Alone in the darkened compartment, the explorers huddled together just inside the open doorway to the back room. This gave them a clear view of the front counter without being in the way. The

spy would most likely search the drawers and cabinets in the drop-off area and would ignore the oddly shaped mound of laundry nearby. That was their hope, at least.

Cruz heard the click of a latch.

"Someone's coming!" gasped Lani.

The door slowly opened. The light from the passage illuminated a head and shoulders. The spy! He padded in and gently shut the door.

Cruz's heart began to race. He broke out in a cold sweat. He could hear drawers opening and closing. Clever. The spy wasn't going to turn on the lights. Still, wasn't it hard to look for a small stone in the dark?

"Can't tell who it is." Lani's voice was a wisp of air. "He's wearing a cap or something on his head. That's all I can see. I think he activated his shadow badge."

"Great," hissed Emmett. "We're all camouflaged?"

"We've got to see his face," whispered Sailor. "I'll tiptoe over there."

"Be careful," said Cruz.

"That's my middle name."

Several minutes passed. The spy was still rifling through drawers. However, he was nearing the end of the counter. If they didn't ID him soon . . .

Something zipped across Cruz's path. Was that Sailor? If it was, she was awfully close to the—

Thump.

"Ouch!" It *was* Sailor.

The door was opening. The spy was getting away!

Cruz leaped to his feet, slapping his hands against the wall to find light. He flipped the switch and was immediately blinded. Shielding his face, Cruz blinked away the spots in front of him in time to see the door swing shut. Meanwhile, Sailor was on the floor. She'd fallen over a laundry cart. Lani flew to the door. She flung it open, her head ping-ponging as she searched the passage. "He's gone," she groaned. "We're too close to the stairs. He could have gone up or down." Lani went to help Sailor. "You okay?"

"Yeah." Sailor got to her feet, rubbing her hip. "Guess I'd better change my middle name."

"Did you get a look at him?" Lani asked her.

"No. I was trying to move to the side when I smacked into the cart." Sailor limped toward Cruz. "You?"

He shook his head. "Sorry, Lani. We're not very good spy catchers."

"I'm not so hot either," said Lani. "I didn't figure he'd keep the lights off. I don't know how he could see a thing in the dark."

"Night-vision glasses," came the cool reply.

Three heads turned to the orange, thawing snowman unwrapping a towel from his head. "I have 'em, too," continued Emmett. In the two seconds it took for him to slide his glasses up the bridge of his nose, they changed from buttery yellow to grass green to bright turquoise. "Did I ever tell you that? I mean, I figured as long as I was creating emotion-sensing glasses, they might as well magnify stuff *and* see at night—"

"Emmett!" snapped Cruz. "Can you ID the spy or not?"

A shadow crossed Emmett's face. "I can," he croaked.

Cruz, Lani, and Sailor froze.

"Well?" burst Sailor. "Who was it?"

"Felipe," Emmett sad sadly. "It was Felipe."

"FELIPE RIVERA, A NEBULA SPY?" Sailor paced the length of Lani's veranda. "I cannot believe it."

Cruz couldn't either. Felipe was a friend. And a good guy. Or so he'd thought.

After the spy had left the laundry compartment, the four of them had hurried back to Lani's cabin to discuss what had happened.

Lani glanced at Cruz. "Your mystery friend did say, 'the spy is closer than you think.' You can't get much closer than the boy who lives next door."

"And Felipe *is* into spy gadgets in a big way," reminded Sailor.

"You're sure it was Felipe?" Cruz pressed his roommate. "I mean, if he had on a cap and night-vision goggles, maybe—"

"These weren't our Academy standard-issue goggles," broke in Emmett. "I could tell by the shape they were the new OptiTek 5000s. Felipe got them for Christmas. He's very protective of them. Wouldn't even let me look at them."

Even Cruz had to admit that was some pretty good evidence against Felipe. Still, he wanted to be positive. "We should start feeding him some false information and see if he passes it along to Nebula," said Cruz.

"We're going to the Taj Mahal this weekend," said Lani. "We could try some misdirection. You could tell him you're going to see relatives in . . . I don't know . . . Madagascar?"

Cruz liked that idea. His travel would not be considered unusual. The explorers were allowed to leave the ship occasionally on weekends to visit friends and family. They had to have permission from their parents and Taryn, of course, who required the particulars of where they were headed, who they were staying with, and when they'd be returning.

"Be sure to say it's your *mom's* relatives," added Emmett. "That'll really keep Nebula guessing."

"It's a good start," said Sailor with a mischievous grin, "but turn-about is fair play, too."

"What do you mean?" asked Cruz

"She means we should spy on the spy," said Emmett.

"We could use my acousticks if you want," said Lani. "We could hear him from inside my cabin, no problem."

"I could hack into his OS band and tablet," volunteered Emmett. He tapped the corner of his glasses. "And from our veranda, my magnification feature could come in handy."

"Cracker!" exclaimed Sailor. "This is going to be great."

Cruz wasn't so sure. Misdirecting Felipe in order to throw Nebula off their trail was one thing, but snooping into the lives of the other explorers? That was entirely different. Cruz leaned against the rail. He looked out at the silvery blue ocean. A half-moon glowed pale gray in the sky, its reflection on the water lighting a path for *Orion* to follow. It also lit up the ship's observatory. Someone had come to stand at the curved window that jutted over the stern. It was Bryndis. The moon must have caught her attention, too.

"Cruz?" Lani was next to him. "Something wrong?"

"I was … wondering," he said. "If we use your acousticks to eavesdrop on Felipe, won't you hear the conversations of other explorers, too?"

"Yeah, I guess …" She lifted a shoulder, as if to say that was the price that had to be paid.

Cruz looked at Emmett. "And it's not just Felipe's room you'd be looking into, you know. It's Kwento's, too."

His roommate fidgeted, his glasses becoming a concerned gray-blue. Everyone leaned on the rail. They gazed out at the ocean in silence. Cruz hadn't meant to throw cold water on things.

Cruz rubbed his eyes. He didn't want to think about Felipe or spies or Nebula anymore tonight. Glancing up, he saw that Bryndis was slowly walking the perimeter of the observatory. How he wished he were up there with her.

If he hurried, he could be …

Cruz backed up to the balcony door, feeling for the knob. "Uh . . . guys? Can we talk about this later?"

Sailor tipped her head to signal for him to go.

Cruz raced up the three flights to the bridge deck. He hurried down the passage past the library and into the observatory. Catching his breath, his eyes swept across the cherrywood-paneled room, from the long wall of antique navigational instruments to the river rock fire-place to the greenhouse. The compartment was empty.

Cruz was about to leave when movement caught his eye. Something was sticking out from beyond the arm of a leather sofa in a little nook on the other side of the fireplace. A foot! Stepping toward it, he saw her. Bryndis had her head down. She was reading. An elbow and her tablet rested on a thick, padded armrest. Next to the sofa, a floor lamp with a teardrop shade made up of a million tiny triangles of glass cast a kaleidoscope of colors onto her light blond head.

"Hi," he said quietly, not wanting to startle her.

Bryndis looked up. "Uh . . . h-hi." She hesitated for a moment, then touched the spot next to her, inviting him to sit.

"Looks like you got the place all to yourself." He sank onto the edge of the cushion.

"Já."

Cruz tapped his fingertips together.

She clicked her tongue.

He stared at the greenhouse door.

She stared at her tablet.

Is it warm in here?

Bryndis tucked her hair behind her ear. "Guess you noticed I've been avoiding you, huh?"

"A little." He tried to say it like it was no big deal. But it was, of course.

"Sorry about that. You're off the hook. That's the right phrase in English, isn't it?"

He wrinkled his brow. "It is, but ..."

What exactly was he off the hook for?

"You have tons in common," said Bryndis. "I can see why you would ..."

Why he would *what*? What *was* she talking about? This was harder than trying to break one of Aunt Marisol's codes!

Bryndis was still talking, though her voice seemed to be getting smaller with each word. He had to lean in to hear her. "... plus, Lani is smart and nice. And fun, too. I love the silver stripe in her hair."

Whoa! Whoa! Did she say ...?

Cruz smacked a palm to his chest. "You think Lani and me ... that I ... that we ...?"

"I wasn't sure ... until Mahé." Lashes shaded her blue eyes. "When she came up over the hill after rescuing Professor Gabriel ... the look on your face ... the way you hugged her. It was so obvious that Lani and you—"

"No! Bryndis, you're wrong ... about Lani and me ... I ... I mean, you're right but you're wrong," he stumbled. "We *do* have a connection, but not the one you think. She's my best friend from back home."

She tipped her head. "Best ... friend?"

"We've known each other since we were eight years old," he rushed on. "We both applied to the Academy, but only I got in. After Renshaw was expelled, Dr. Hightower invited the next person on the list of alternates to come to the Academy. That was Lani. None of us knew she was an alternate, not even Lani. Dr. Hightower keeps the list a secret. When Lani showed up to meet us in Turkey, I was completely surprised. It was my idea to pretend we didn't know each other," said Cruz. "I didn't want anyone thinking that Lani had gotten special treatment. She's here because she deserves to be."

"Best friends!" Bryndis let out a happy sigh. "I only wish I would have known."

"I wanted to tell you."

There were some other things he wanted to tell her, too, and now that he knew Bryndis wasn't the spy, he could. He could trust her. He could tell her everything.

Bryndis's head was moving toward him. Suddenly, her lips were touching his. He tasted coconut lip balm. Softness. Warmth. Cruz felt dizzy, but not like any dizzy he'd ever known. It was like being on the highest, fastest, twistiest roller coaster on Earth. His brain and heart and stomach were all switching places. He was a jumbled mess of terror and joy. And guts.

As quickly as the ride had begun it was over. Their lips parted. Cruz sat back, waiting for equilibrium to return. He was breathless. Weightless. And, strangely, fearless.

She let out a laugh.

Uncertain, Cruz drew back. He had never kissed a girl. Had he done it wrong?

"I was thinking," said Bryndis, "good thing you don't get a lemonade bath after your first kiss."

Cruz grinned. "Yeah, good thing."

She reached for his hand, weaving her fingers in his. "Thanks for telling me about Lani."

"So, we're okay?"

Her dimples appeared. "We're okay."

Funny thing about going on the highest, fastest, twistiest roller coaster on Earth: It'll completely scare the beans out of you. Yet the minute you step off, you can't wait to go again.

14

AFGHAN.
PAKISTAN
CHINA
BHUTAN
NEPAL
AGRA, INDIA
INDIA
MYANMAR
(BURMA)
Arabian
Sea
THAILAND
Bay of
Bangel
MALDIVES
SRI LANKA
INDODESIA

▶ **CRUZ, EMMETT,** Lani, and Sailor
stood shoulder to shoulder, staring at the grand ivory tomb in the
distance. Cruz's gaze traveled up the soaring arches, onion domes, and
pointed spires. He had never seen anything like it. The Taj Mahal was
spectacular.

A minaret framed each corner of a platform that supported the
building just the way they did on Aunt Marisol's charm. In real life, however, the tomb's marble support structure was 20 feet high! Also con-
structed with marble bricks, each minaret stretched at least 100 feet
into the air. Cruz zeroed in on the minaret on the back right—the
northeast one. From here, it looked no different from the others. He
remembered how Lani had said the minarets were built at an angle to
tilt slightly away from the tomb, but Cruz couldn't tell that by looking
at them.

A manicured garden several football fields in length stood between
the south gate the explorers had come through and the tomb. In the
center of the garden, the building's impressive domes and spires were
captured in the reflection of a long, rectangular pond. On each side of
the waters, a row of cedar trees and a path of red bricks led to the
tomb's platform.

"Let's go," said Cruz, sliding the sprocket-shaped sunglasses from his
head to rest on his nose. Under a milky sky, tinted rosy peach by the

late afternoon sun, Cruz led the way down the brick path to the left of the pond. He hit the globe pin on his uniform and requested information. His friends did the same. Dodging tourists, they read what appeared in their sunglasses.

The Taj Mahal, meaning "crown of the palaces," is considered one of the seven wonders of the modern world. It was built by Mughal emperor Shah Jahan in the 17th century as the final resting place for his beloved wife Mumtaz Mahal. Shah Jahan is also buried here. It took 20,000 laborers and artists 22 years to complete construction on the marble tomb, gardens, and complex. The building changes colors depending on the time of day. It takes on a pink hue in the morning, turns white in the evening, and appears gold under moonlight. Every year, millions of tourists visit this architectural jewel of India on the southern bank of the Yamuna River.

Emmett scooted out of the way a second before a stroller would have rolled over his foot. "Looks like all of those millions of tourists decided to come today," he said.

Once they reached the end of the path, they paused to slip on the required shoe covers, then went through the lower door of the platform and up a flight of steps. The stairwell opened to the front of the tomb. The building was even more beautiful up close. Around the arched entryway and each of the windows, scarlet red and hunter green polished stones had been inlaid in the marble in the shapes of flowers and vines. The information on the explorers' sunglasses revealed it was a technique called *parchin kari*. Delicate calligraphy flowed down the walls. Thin corner columns were inlaid with dark stone in rows to create a horizontal zigzag pattern.

Their papery soles sliding over the white marble platform, the explorers made a beeline for the back corner. The minarets were set apart from the four corners of the building by about 30 feet or so. Each tower was divided into three equal sections by balconies. The top balcony was topped with a spired dome. Reaching the northeast tower, Cruz saw that the bottom was covered with carvings. A row of grape leaves wrapped the top edge of the octagonal base. Beneath the leaves were long rectangular panels filled with various swirls and flourishes. A trio of small marble steps led to a pair of white wooden doors. A heavy chain wove through the door handles. It was held in place by three padlocks.

Emmett let out a heavy sigh. "Well, we can't hack into those."

"We couldn't have hacked into *anything*," corrected Sailor.

Due to security, they'd only been allowed to bring in their cell phones, MC cameras, and water. They'd had to leave their tablets and backpacks at the security checkpoint.

The explorers studied the marble tower. The padlocked door was the only way in.

"What about the key your mom left?" whispered Sailor.

Cruz had brought it along, as well as the other things from his mother's box that he thought he might need: the two washers, the pad of cat sticky notes, and his photo with the swirl cipher. Cruz didn't need to take the key from his pocket to know it wouldn't work. He did anyway, though, to show Sailor that it was far too small for the clunky locks.

Sailor's face fell.

"We're not beat yet," Cruz said. He had a backup plan. Unzipping his pocket, he said softly, "Mell, on."

"Your trusty assistant." Sailor brightened. "How could I have forgotten?"

When the drone came to shoulder level, Cruz said quietly, "Mell, please open these three locks." He took a quick peek behind them to be sure the coast was still clear before saying, "Mell, go."

The honeybee zipped into the bottom lock. She opened it in less than 10 seconds, then immediately flew into the middle lock.

"Mell to the rescue again," said Emmett. "If it wasn't for her, we wouldn't have survived our first week at the Academy."

A shiver ripped through Cruz's spine. They never did find out which of Nebula's agents had tried to kill them by trapping them in a supply closet and pumping in poisonous gas. He sure hoped it wasn't Felipe!

The second lock took Mell about half a minute to unlatch. With a quick glance at Cruz, the MAV flew into the top lock.

"Last one," said Lani, clasping her hands.

One minute passed. Then two.

"Give her time," said Cruz, watching Sailor's grin fade.

Finally, after five minutes, Mell appeared. Flying to Cruz, she flashed her gold eyes. It meant she had not been able to complete her mission. She couldn't open the lock. The bee dropped her head.

"It's all right, Mell," soothed Cruz. "Two out of three isn't bad. Thanks for trying." He expanded his pocket and instructed her to go in. "Mell, off."

"What now?" whispered Sailor.

"There has to be a secret way in," said Lani, her eyes roving up the marble bricks.

"It probably has a locking mechanism," said Emmett, "like the bird-fish symbol at Petra."

"Maybe that's what the 1-1-2-9 is for." Sailor dipped her head toward the base of the minaret. "It could be embedded in the scrollwork."

"We've got to take a closer look," said Cruz.

A thin rope strung between several posts around the column and a sign that read PLEASE KEEP DISTANCE FROM RAILING made it clear no one was allowed behind the tower. However, this was an emergency.

"Emmett and I can cover you, Cruz, while Sailor and you check it out," said Lani. She took out her phone and posed in front of the minaret, pretending to take a selfie. "Come on, Emmett," she muttered.

He followed her lead.

Sailor motioned that she would go around the tower clockwise, leaving Cruz to head counterclockwise.

They waited until a family with kids went by, then stepped over the rope. Only a few feet separated the back of the minaret from the three-foot marble wall at the edge of the platform. Sliding into the space, Cruz got to work. First, he scanned the marble bricks for the date of his birthday, going from the bottom to as high as he could reach on his toes. He didn't see any numbers. Next, he searched for loose bricks, pressing on each one and sliding his fingers along the seams made of black stone that joined the slabs. He inspected the row of grape leaves that ran along the perimeter of the base, along with the raised scroll-work panels beneath it. Still, he found nothing. Cruz met Sailor coming the other way. She was poking, prodding, and pushing things, too.

"I didn't find anything," he said. "You?"

"Nope."

They went over the rope to deliver the bad news to Lani and Emmett.

"I know we're in the right spot," said Cruz. "What are we missing?"

The four of them stared up at the tower, as if somehow the answer would magically float down to them. All Cruz got for his trouble was a stiff neck.

The rosy ball in the sky was hanging low. The monument would be closing in a half hour.

"Maybe we overlooked something in the clue," said Lani.

"We could go back to the B&B and watch it again," suggested Emmett. "We've got one more day here."

Dr. Hightower had arranged for them to stay with Professor Sunita Kumari, a friend of hers who taught at the local university and whose family ran Dayaalu, a bed-and-breakfast outside of Agra. They'd dropped their bags off at the guesthouse before taking an Auto Auto to the historic site.

"That's a good idea," said Sailor. "We'll look at the clue and come back tomorrow."

Cruz hesitated. He didn't want to leave the Taj Mahal, but what else could he do? He let Sailor guide him away from the minaret, yet kept looking back, hoping an idea, solution, or revelation would strike. None did. At the platform steps, the explorers tugged off their shoe covers and began the long walk through the garden to the south gate.

Cruz lagged behind his friends. Maybe if he went back to the beginning, he could figure out where he'd made a wrong turn. His mother's clue had led him to her box of things, which contained Aunt Marisol's Aztec crown charm.

Something about that had been tugging at him. Cruz didn't get why his mother had chosen *that* charm. It would have made more sense to take the Taj Mahal charm, which *was* the third charm on Aunt Marisol's bracelet, and engrave *NE MINARET 1-1-2-9* on the back of it.

What was so special about the crown?

Crown.

It *was* his last name. Coronado was Spanish for "crowned." What else? Taj Mahal meant "crown of the palaces." Was that his mom's way of saying she wanted him to look for a crown here? He hadn't seen anything that resembled a crown on the minaret.

A hand locked on to his elbow. "Keep walking."

It was the mysterious blond girl from Petra! He would never forget how she had pushed him out of the way seconds before a rockslide had come crashing down, then vanished before he could even get her name.

"What are you doing here?" he hissed.

"Trying to save your life," she said, her English accent crisp. "Again."

Lani, Sailor, and Emmett were about 20 feet ahead, their heads together as they strolled. Deep in conversation, they hadn't noticed that Cruz was no longer with them.

Still holding his elbow, the girl looked straight ahead. She was wearing jeans and a pink sweater over a white tee. She had a blue backpack with white polka dots slung over her shoulder. "I'm the one who's been sending you anonymous notes."

"*You?*" Cruz shook his head. She'd taken him by surprise. "Who are you, anyway?"

"My name is Roewyn. My father is the head of"—releasing his arm, she turned, finally, to look at him—"Nebula Pharmaceuticals."

Cruz gawked. "You mean, your *dad* is—"

"Out to destroy your mom's cipher. And you, if he can." She rubbed a finger over her lips as if to erase the words she'd spoken. "Lucky for you, Mr. Prescott and the others that work for my dad—"

"Prescott. Is he the one in the snakeskin cowboy boots?"

She gave a nod, along with an eye roll.

At last, a name to match to the assassin.

"Anyway, they keep messing up," continued Roewyn. "They were supposed to deal with you before you turned thirteen, but—"

"Why?" Cruz pounced. "Why thirteen?"

"Don't you know?"

"No." He could tell that was not the response she'd expected. "I'm looking for my mom's cipher. That's what they're after, like you said. It has nothing to do with me."

"You're wrong. It has everything to do with you." The warm evening breeze wrapped her hair around her neck. She lifted a hand to untangle it. "Something else is going on. You scare my father, and nothing scares him."

Cruz didn't understand. Except for searching for his mom's formula, he wasn't a threat to anybody.

"Did you figure out yet who's the explorer spy?" she pressed.

Still wary of her, he said, "I... I'm not sure. Do *you* know?"

"No. My father uses code names to protect the identities of those who work for him. My dad's code name is Lion. Thorne Prescott is Cobra. He's the only one I know by name. Jaguar and Zebra are on board *Orion*. There's another one, too. Meerkat. All I know about him is that he tried to hurt you back at the Academy."

Mr. Rook! She was talking about former Academy librarian Malcolm Rook. He was Meerkat.

"Meerkat no longer works for my father. Watch out for him," she warned. "My dad discovered that Meerkat is trying to get to the next piece of the cipher before you do."

"*What?*" This was getting crazier by the minute.

"One of the spies on board *Orion* is a double agent and working with Meerkat. Cobra could be a double agent, too. That's why I'm here. I had to be absolutely sure no one would intercept my message."

Cruz was confused. "Which spy is working for who?"

"It doesn't matter. All you need to know is that you are in more danger now than ever." Roewyn looked over Cruz's shoulder. "Meerkat or Cobra could be following you. So could another one of my dad's agents. I... I don't always know what he's planning."

Cruz's head spun, searching for a head with wavy red hair or a pair of snakeskin-print cowboy boots. He didn't see either. The light was beginning to fade and Lani, Emmett, and Sailor had finally realized that

Cruz wasn't with them. And that someone else was. His friends were rushing back.

Roewyn saw them, too. "I have to go."

"Wait!" It was his turn to reach for her arm. "You said there were *two* spies on board *Orion*."

"That's right. Jaguar is the explorer. Zebra's an adult—I think. That's how I knew you'd be here. They report to my father, and I ... well, I have good ears." She backed away.

"I ... I don't get it." He wanted to believe her. "Why are you doing this?"

Roewyn shook her head. "What happened to your mom's work ... to her ... it's not what my great-grandmother would have wanted for the company she founded. Someone in the family has to make things right, and I'm the only one who can."

"Won't your dad be angry if he finds out what you're doing?"

"Which is why he can never find out. Watch your back, Cruz. More rockslides are coming, if you know what I mean."

He did.

Turning onto one of the side paths, Roewyn hurried away seconds before Emmett, Sailor, and Lani got there.

Cruz filled them in on their conversation. When he finished, Sailor let out a groan. "I was hoping we'd seen the last of Mr. Rook."

"And Prescott," added Lani.

"I don't like it." Emmett's emoto-glasses were dark purple half-moons of suspicion. "She traveled a long way to save somebody she doesn't even know."

"Twice," said Sailor.

"She said it had something to do with her great-grandmother's company," said Cruz.

"I'm with Emmett on this," said Lani. "Roewyn said she had to be sure she found you. If Felipe told Nebula that you were going to Madagascar and Zebra told them it was India, showing up here she had a fifty-fifty chance of being right. That's hardly being *sure*."

Cruz lifted a shoulder. "Maybe she's a good guesser?"

"Or a good liar," shot Emmett.

That sent goose bumps down Cruz's arms. But he saw what Emmett was getting at. Maybe Roewyn was being honest with him and maybe she wasn't. At the moment, however, Roewyn wasn't what was most worrying him. It was that second spy. Zebra could be a teacher, a staff member, a crewman, or a security officer. Faces flashed through his brain. Chef Kristos. Dr. Eikenboom. Dr. Holland. Jericho Miles. Even Emmett's mom. It could be *anyone*.

The last bit of sunlight was fading. They had to go.

Walking up the steps to the gate, Cruz stuffed his hands in his pockets and felt a wisp of paper slip through his fingers. He pulled out the photo of himself as a child, laughing through a grape juice mustache. Life was so much easier when you were a kid.

Cruz turned the picture over. And there it was.

The solution. The answer. The revelation.

"Guys!" cried Cruz. "We have to go back!"

15

▶ **"RATTLE YOUR DAGS,**

people," huffed Sailor, jogging down the red stone path.

"Huh?" Racing beside her, Cruz pumped his arms to gain speed.

"Hurry! They're going to close."

"I know! I know!"

Lani sprinted past them both.

Pulling up at the entrance to the platform, the four explorers threw on their shoe covers, scrambled up the steps, and hurried across the platform to the northeast minaret.

"What's going on?" panted Emmett, the last one to arrive at the tower. His emoto-glasses were a violent storm of colors and shapes.

Thrusting the back of the photo in front of his friend's face, Cruz nodded to the raised scrollwork on the base of the tower. "I think somewhere among these carvings are the swirls that stand for 1-1-2-9 in Mom's code."

"What are you waiting for?" Sailor gave Cruz a push. "Go!"

Hurtling the rope, Cruz scooted into the cramped space between the tower and the back wall. He fell to his knees and began running his hands over the marble. The swirls had to be here. They *just* had to! Halfway around the column, however, he was starting to wonder if he'd been wrong. None of the scrollwork looked like his mom's cipher.

"Cruz!" It was Sailor. "Security!"

Cruz tried to pick up the pace, but his palms were sweaty. His hands kept slipping. Plus, he couldn't go *too* fast or he'd miss the cipher. He was losing sunlight. Cruz hoped that fingertips could find what his eyes were struggling to see.

There! His thumb had rolled over a clockwise curve. It was raised a bit higher than the others. Cruz followed the curl to its end, felt a break, then a dot. He knew this swirl! It was code for the number one. Cruz moved his hand to the right. The next curlicue was identical to the first symbol. Another numeral one. His pulse quickened. The next symbol was a slightly longer clockwise swirl. And a dot. That was a two. And finally, a short counterclockwise swirl with a dot at the bottom. Nine. 1-1-2-9!

"The mausoleum will be closing," he heard a man say on the other side of the tower. "You'll need to start for an exit."

"Thanks. We're leaving now for the parking lot," Emmett said loudly, clearly for Cruz's benefit.

Hunched behind the tower, Cruz stayed put until he no longer heard voices or footsteps. He started to click on the light on his OS band, then thought better of it. It was too bright. Someone might see. He opened his jacket pocket. "Mell, on," he whispered.

A pair of golden eyes blinked up at him.

"Mell, turn your eyes to low and come on out. Stay close to my hands."

She obeyed. With a quick check to make sure he was alone, Cruz placed his fingertips on the swirls, now bathed in Mell's golden glow. One tip to each swirl—pinkie to index finger. He took a full breath and then ... pushed.

Cruz lifted his hand. Was the dim light playing tricks on him or were the raised swirls beginning to flatten? He bent until his nose was practically touching marble. He was right. The swirls *were* disappearing! Within seconds the marble where the cipher had been was completely smooth. It was as if they had never been there at all!

Cruz heard a rumble. At first, he thought it was thunder. He tipped his head back and saw stars glittering through a wispy layer of clouds.

He felt a vibration. Something was happening within the tower. The marble panel was separating from the base! Cruz drew back as the entire panel slid to his left. A hot breeze blasted his face. The slab stopped, revealing a hole beneath the base of the minaret. A secret chamber!

It was big enough for a person to fit through.

"Have a look, Mell," said Cruz with more courage than he felt.

The drone flew into the opening, her eyes illuminating a flight of steep marble steps with no railing. Leaning into the gap, Cruz peered down. The steps descended into darkness. Cruz pulled back. He was apprehensive. After all, his last cave adventure had nearly cost him his life.

Mell was waiting. She tilted her head as if to ask, *Are we going or not?*

He sighed. "Yeah, we're going."

Glancing back to make sure no one was waiting to give him a shove, he took off his shoe covers. Cruz went through the gap feetfirst, scooting in on his rear. It wasn't pretty, but it was safe. He crab-walked down one step, then two. So far, so good. On the third step, he got slowly to his feet. A bead of sweat rolled down his temple. His OS band indicated the temperature inside the chamber was 88.3 degrees. Cruz wasn't too worried. He knew his uniform would help regulate his body temperature, though he wished he hadn't left his water with Emmett.

Cruz heard another peal of thunder.

The panel was closing! He whirled around, one foot sliding off the edge of the steps. Cruz had to throw out his arms to keep from toppling over the side. By the time he regained his balance—

Boom!

He was sealed in.

Cruz searched for swirls, levers, buttons—anything that might open the panel, but there was nothing. He searched the darkness below. "Guess we're going down, Mell."

By the amber glow of the honeybee's eyes, Cruz gingerly began making his way down the stairs. "You can turn your lights on high now,

Mell," he instructed. "I don't think we're in danger of being seen."

She bumped up the light level, revealing even more steps.

"Emmett Lu to Cruz Coronado."

Cruz was surprised to hear a voice coming through his comm pin. "Cruz, here. Emmett, can you hear me?"

"Loud and clear."

"I thought our comm pins had a range of—" He had been about to say they had a 25-mile radius from the ship but remembered Fanchon had said the range could be boosted. She had already done it once for him, in Iceland. *Thanks again, Fanchon!*

"We're in the Auto Auto in the parking lot," said Sailor. "Where are you?"

"Inside the minaret."

"You *were* right!"

"The swirls opened a panel at the base of the tower. I'm in a secret chamber, heading down a staircase." He wiped away the sweat beading on his forehead. "It's like an oven in here. My OS band reads 92.8 degrees. And that's not my body temp."

"Do you have any water?" asked Sailor.

"No."

"Better keep the comm link open so you can give us the play-by-play," said Emmett.

Several dozen steps later, Cruz hit solid ground. "I've reached the bottom," he reported. The ceiling was so low, Cruz could touch it when he lifted his arm. "It's a small room carved out of solid rock." He followed Mell's light as she flew the perimeter. "I'd say it's about twice the size of our cabin on *Orion*. There's nothing here. It's completely empt— Hold on ... Mell's got something."

The bee was tapping her front legs on glass. Cruz had mistaken a reflection for stone.

"There's a dark window ... or some kind of glass wall behind the stairs," he described. "I don't see a doorknob." Thinking he might be able to slide the pane aside, he placed his left palm against it. "Whoa!"

he shouted. "My hand went right through the wall! It's crazy. It feels like ... like gel."

"Watch it," warned Emmett. "You never know with a shape-shifting material, especially if it's hot down there. The panel is probably operating on a macroscopic level using liquid crystal elastomers, and the stimulus is likely heat ..."

While Emmett talked, Cruz tried to retrieve his hand. As he did, something clamped around his wrist. It was cold. And metal. And tight. He felt a tug. Then another. Something was trying to drag him through the gel wall!

"... so it could oscillate." Emmett was still talking. "You know, change back and forth between a hard and soft material, based on its molecular structure and the temperature in the grotto. Oh, and your body heat ..."

"Good to ... know," grunted Cruz, trying to yank his arm out of the cuff. But the more he pulled, the more it tightened. He was losing ground, inch by inch. About to surrender his elbow to the black wall, Cruz cried out, "Argggh!"

As suddenly as the pressure began, it was gone. The quick release sent Cruz stumbling. He no longer felt anything around his wrist, but he wasn't out of trouble yet.

"Cruz, what's happening?" demanded Sailor.

"Uh ... the gel hardened ... unfortunately, with half my arm stuck on the other side."

"Told ya," sighed Emmett. "Congealment is likely heat-based."

"It's roasting in here and there aren't any windows to open," huffed Cruz. "Not that I could reach them if there were ..."

Bzzzz. Mell was next to him. Cruz was glad to see she hadn't been sucked through the wall, too.

Cruz's arm was starting to go numb. He was about to drop to his knees when an image appeared on the glass. It was a photograph of his double-helix birthmark. However, the mark was on a smaller arm, and one without an OS band. He recognized that arm. It was his! The photo must have been taken when he was much younger, maybe four or five years old. Another picture appeared next to it. This one showed his wrist as it was now, with an OS band covering part of the pinkish red twisted ladder on his skin. The camera had been able to penetrate the filmy band, enhancing the section of his birthmark that the band had hidden.

MATCH. The word blinked in green letters below the pair of photos. MATCH. MATCH.

As Cruz studied the two images, the glass began to wobble. The gel was loosening. The wall began to turn liquid. It fell to the ground in blobs of dark goo.

Cruz rubbed his sore wrist. "It must be some kind of biometric identification system. Looks like I passed." At his feet, the liquid was

evaporating. He watched it vanish. "Too bad I can't take a sample back. Fanchon would love this stuff."

Cruz carefully stepped over where the wall had been. Ahead and to his right was more rock. Both were dead ends. To his left, Cruz saw ...

"Oh no!"

"What is it?" asked Emmett.

"Another gel wall."

"Don't touch it!" yelled his friends.

"Don't worry." More sweat was trickling down his neck. Cruz checked his OS band. The temperature was 96.1. This time, when Cruz approached the dark panel, a touch keyboard appeared on its shiny surface. Above the keyboard, Cruz saw a row of a half dozen horizontal lines. "Uh-oh. Looks like I don't have a choice. I have to touch this one," he said into his comm pin. "It wants a password. Six letters."

"Sailor!" blurted Sailor.

"Hardly," snapped Emmett. "Unless Cruz's mom could predict the future."

Cruz could almost see Sailor roll her eyes, but Emmett was right. Cruz's mom had established the password more than seven years ago, so it couldn't refer to anything from the present. Cruz's first name had two few letters. His last name too many. Marco, Marisol, and Petra wouldn't work. Neither would crown, charm, Synthesis, formula, helix, or journal.

"Anybody have anything?" asked Cruz.

He got no response.

"Cruz to Emmett Lu? Sailor? Lani?"

He had lost their signal.

Cruz's MAV came to land on his shoulder. "You're two letters and a few years short, Mell," he kidded. "Mom would have liked you. You could have helped her come up with a bee or insect cipher."

Cipher! That had six letters. Using a light touch, in case something was on the other side of this wall, Cruz typed C-I-P-H-E-R into the spaces. Instantly, the letters turned red. A few seconds later, they vanished. The shape-shifting wall didn't so much as wobble.

Cruz's core was cool, thanks to his uniform, but his hands and feet were on fire. His head was, too. Cruz's mouth was dry and his stomach was grumbling to be fed. He leaned back against the side of the rock wall and slid down slowly to sit on the ground. He needed a minute to rest. Pressing his comm pin, he tried contacting Emmett, Sailor, and Lani again. No luck. Cruz tried his phone, too, even though he was likely too deep to get a signal out. He was right.

Cruz stared up at the black wall with its six blank spaces and keyboard. What was he supposed to do now? Cruz couldn't go forward and he couldn't go back. It was getting harder and harder to breathe in the sweltering grotto. He glanced at his OS band: 103.2.

Cruz wished he had his silver holo-dome. Seeing his mom and dad together always brought him comfort. And a cold, windy beach sounded good about now. Truth was, Cruz didn't need the dome. He'd watched the video it contained thousands and thousands of times. He knew every word, every look, every frame by heart.

Cruz put a hand to his shoulder. "Mell, off," he said, his voice raspy.

Her gold eyes went dark.

The air growing thin, and his head getting foggy, Cruz closed his eyes. He let his mind wander to a rocky shore from long ago.

16

►**CHUNKS OF WET** gray sand flew in all directions. At the surf's edge, the toddler in a yellow duck raincoat and matching hat was busy bulldozing a trench around himself.

Watching him fearlessly plunge his red shovel into the sand, his mother laughed. "Look at him dig, Marco." Gray-blue eyes peered directly into the camera. "Our budding archaeologist."

"And you were so hoping he'd go into neurobiology," said his dad from behind the lens.

"He can do both." She turned to her son. "You can do anything you set your mind to, Cruzer."

Realizing he was trapped on an island of his own creation, the boy held out his arms. "Mama, help!"

His mother bent to fold him into herself.

The scene went dark.

Cruz's eyelids flew open. That was it!

He was still in the grotto. Still thirsty. Still hungry. Still roasting. But now he had a password.

"Come on!" he said, willing himself to his feet. Cruz stumbled to the touch-screen keyboard and typed C-R-U-Z-E-R.

Please let this one work. It's my last chance.

Through the haze of heat and fatigue, Cruz watched the word turn green. The wall was quivering. The gel began to liquefy. Clumps of black goo fell to the ground. He'd done it! Cruz had given the computer the correct password.

Wiping his brow, he trudged through the evaporating substance. Ahead and to the right, he saw only stone. To his left, Cruz anticipated another shiny, dark wall but instead was met with a barrier of solid rock. A nook was carved into the wall at chest level and a spotlight from above illuminated an oval cedar box. There was no biometric ID panel. No screen demanding a password. Not even a lock on the box. It seemed awfully easy. Unless ...

There was something inside the box, guarding the cipher, like a black mamba or a bunch of deathstalker scorpions.

Cruz edged toward the nook. His eyes darted from the ground to the ceiling and from side to side, scanning for anything that might slither, pounce, bite, or sting. Sweat dripped from his brow, stinging his eyes. Cruz reached out, his fingers finding the side of the curved lid. "Here we go." He psyched himself up. "Three ... two ... one!"

Cruz flung up the lid, then shielded himself for an attack. None came. He slowly lowered his arms. The box held only one item: an aqua envelope. Cruz crept toward it. He cautiously dipped his hand into the box. Catching the envelope between his thumb and index finger, he lifted it as if it was packed with explosives, which it might very well be. Cruz slid his finger under the flap of the envelope. Half turning and shutting one eye, he eased it upward.

No explosion. *Whew!*

Cruz tilted the square. A smooth black triangle slid into his palm. The fifth cipher.

Had Cruz not been so weak, he would have let out a celebratory whoop. As it was, he could barely attach the new piece to the other four hanging from the lanyard around his neck. His hands shook and it took several tries, but eventually he felt the piece click into place.

Raising his head, Cruz did a double take. Was he hallucinating? In the time it had taken for him to connect the pie-shaped cipher to the other pieces, the box, the nook, and the entire rock wall had disappeared!

Cruz was staring at the same marble steps he had come down. There was one big difference: The stairs were now glowing green.

His thinking was getting pretty foggy, but Cruz thought he had it figured out. He'd started his journey through the grotto behind the steps, and since he'd always made a left turn, three turns had brought him back to where he'd begun. It was an augmented-reality scenario, like the CAVE. Unfortunately, either his mom hadn't set up the climate controls properly or something had malfunctioned. Or maybe Nebula had gotten here first. Unable to get past any of the security measures, they might have found a way to tamper with the atmospheric controls to ensure that Cruz, once in, would never escape.

"Joke's on you . . . Nebula," he rasped.

Cruz began to climb the steps. It was slow going in the heat. He was beat. Cruz bent forward to use his hands to help propel him up the steep staircase the way he had done to climb the massive dunes at Sossusvlei.

Dugan would get a kick out of this, he thought.

Nearing the top, Cruz hit his comm pin. Or tried to. It took him three tries to find it on his lapel. He really was woozy! "Cruz . . . to Emmett Lu."

"Emmett, here! We thought we'd lost you."

"Not . . . yet." Cruz collapsed onto the landing. There, on the side of the wall next to the panel, he could make out four illuminated swirls like those he'd first pressed on the outside of the tower. Glowing gold, they reminded Cruz of the fireworks that spin along the ground and throw off sparks. Cruz tried to push on the twirling wheels, but his brain and hands didn't seem to be in sync. Things were going in and out of focus. He couldn't be sure if he'd made contact.

Cruz heard thunder.

Felt a rush of cool air.

His knees buckled.

The world spun.

A blurry face loomed above him. Cruz started to panic. It could be Rook or Prescott.

He tried to struggle. Tried to scream. But could do neither.

Nebula had won after all.

"It's all right, *hoaaloha*." Lani's face came into view. "I've got you."

"HI, CRUZER."

"Hi, Mom."

It was good to see her. For a while there, he wasn't sure he ever would again.

Cruz was beginning to feel more like himself again. The escape part of the evening was a bit hazy. He remembered Lani helping him to his feet, stumbling through the gate past a surprised security guard, and leaning his head against a cool car window as the Auto Auto drove through a patchwork of farmlands. At Dayaalu Bed and Breakfast, Emmett had brought him some of Dr. Kumari's homemade *chana dal*, a spicy chili-like soup with yellow split chickpeas, tomatoes, and onions. Cruz had rested for an hour or so before gathering his friends to open the holo-journal. Normally, he would have waited to do this until they were safely back on board *Orion*, but with Mr. Rook and Prescott out there trying to get to the cipher ahead of him, he had to be positive that he was holding a genuine piece.

Lani and Sailor were now settled on the pink lotus blossom *kantha* quilt covering the bed. Emmett sat in the corner, consumed by a very big, very pink furry chair. Cruz stood at the end of the bed.

As Cruz looked up at his mother, the video hiccuped—only for a split second, but he caught it. So did his friends. Emmett quickly appeared from the depths of the pink Sasquatch chair. Everyone knew this was a critical moment. Cruz's mom was supposed to inspect the cipher, declare it real, and reveal the next clue. If something went wrong anywhere in this chain of events, it could put Cruz's quest for the formula in jeopardy.

"Mom?" prompted Cruz.

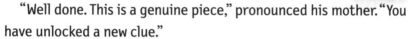

She turned to him. "Do you have the fifth piece of the cipher?"

Whew! That was close.

Cruz held out the slice of black marble. The explorers held their collective breath as they waited for her confirmation. No matter how many times they did this, for Cruz, it never got easier. In fact, it was getting harder. With each new fragment he added to the lanyard, the stakes went higher. He could not afford to make any mistakes now.

"Well done. This is a genuine piece," pronounced his mother. "You have unlocked a new clue."

The explorers relaxed. Cruz grinned at Lani. She had a smudge of dirt on her chin. Emmett and Sailor had told him that the moment Lani had learned that Cruz was inside the secret chamber she'd raced back to the minaret. Lani wouldn't reveal how she'd managed to get inside the Taj Mahal after it had closed. However, based on her dirty palms and the bark stains on the knees of her pants, Cruz deduced some tree climbing had been involved.

"Cruz?" asked his mother. "Are you okay?"

Cruz's jaw dropped. He had expected her to go on to the next clue, as usual. "I ... uh ... uh ..."

"Take it easy," Emmett said quietly. "The bio scan probably analyzes your vital signs or appearance."

Did he look that bad? Cruz smoothed down his hair.

"Might want to answer her," urged Emmett. "We're in uncharted territory here. The sooner we get the program to advance the better."

Cruz cleared his raw throat. "Uh ... I'm all right, Mom."

Petra Coronado tugged on the end of her long blond ponytail, pulling it around to the front of her shoulder. "I'm sorry. I know finding that last cipher must have been difficult but I had to make absolutely sure that you and *only* you would enter the grotto beneath the minaret."

"It's all right. I survived." Cruz held out his arms to prove it. "See? All in one piece. Me, I mean, not the formula." He chuckled nervously. "Not yet."

His mom was looking past him. "I am rushing, I know, but I have to hurry if I am to finish these journal entries in time."

In time. The words sent a chill through Cruz. He'd never heard her admit that Nebula was closing in. Always before it was, *If you find this . . .*

If I'm gone . . .

Now she seemed to be saying, *when.*

When you find this . . .

When I'm gone.

It tore into him. It was as if she already knew how things were going to end.

"You have only three pieces left to find," said his mother. "But do not let your guard down now. The most challenging part of the journey lies ahead."

Cruz stood tall. "I'm ready."

Her eyes narrowed. "I'm sure you think so."

It was spooky. How did she know he was going to say that?

"Before I can unlock the next clue you must answer three questions," said his mother. "Then I will know if you are equipped to continue."

There was a test?

Cruz didn't like this. If he answered incorrectly, she could end his search for the cipher. But what choice did he have? Cruz turned to get some encouragement from his friends. Behind him, Lani, Sailor, and Emmett looked as terrified as he felt. They knew what was on the line here. Everything.

Cruz faced his mother's holo-image and took a deep breath. "O-okay, Mom."

"First question," said his mom. "Has Nebula tried to hurt you?"

This took him by surprise. He'd assumed her questions were going to involve some kind of puzzle he had to solve.

"Um..." Cruz wasn't sure what to say. He knew what she wanted to hear. Should he lie? He gulped hard. "Yes, they have, but I'm all right." He would only expand if she asked him to.

She nodded but showed no indication if he'd given the right answer. "Question two: What is the thing you most fear?"

Oh, wow! How was he supposed to answer that? Cruz was worried about Nebula, of course. Every time he opened the journal, he was scared they wouldn't be able to figure out a clue. He was anxious about doing well at Explorer Academy and not disappointing Aunt Marisol, his dad, Dr. Hightower, and his teachers. And yet...

That wasn't the question, was it? He knew the answer. But could he say it?

Should he say it?

Cruz looked up at her. "The thing I *most* fear"—he licked his lips—"is Dad dying."

Again, she dipped her head, though he thought he saw her face soften a bit this time. "Question three: Name three things right now, at *this very moment*, that make you happy."

Cruz smiled. This was the easiest question of all. "Emmett Lu, Sailor York, and Leilani Kealoha. They are my friends and teammates at Explorer Academy."

A third nod. "Thank you."

"Mom, wait!" Cruz reached out. "I don't know if I gave you the right answers, but... but... I *am* ready to keep looking for the cipher." He had to make her understand. He couldn't quit now. He just couldn't. "Once, a long time ago, you said I could do anything I set my mind to, remember? Do you remember that day at the beach? If you do, if you still believe that, please let me keep going."

She did not respond. Her image appeared to be frozen.

"Mom?" squeaked Cruz.

"She's processing," whispered Emmett from Cruz's left.

Cruz had been so focused on the holo-video he hadn't realized Sailor,

Emmett, and Lani had come to stand beside him.

"Whatever's happening in there was programmed seven years ago," said Emmett. "There's nothing we can do now but hope that Cruz triggered it to continue."

All eyes were riveted to the opaque figure beaming from the journal. The only sound was the ticking of the antique brass clock on the wall next to Cruz.

What was taking so long? The wait was agony.

Cruz *had* to know. Would his mother let him continue searching for the cipher? Or would everything he had fought for, sacrificed for, and nearly died for, end here and now?

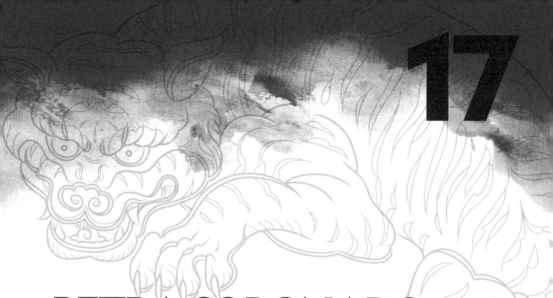

17

▶**PETRA CORONADO** squared
her shoulders.

Cruz's heart was pummeling his chest. Here it came—her decision.

Gray-blue eyes found his. "I believe you answered each question truthfully. Your honesty and courage have proven you are prepared to continue your mission. To find the sixth cipher, journey to the..."

"Wahooooo!" Cruz threw his hands up.

Lani, Sailor, and Emmett were cheering, too.

"Great job!" Sailor flung an arm around Cruz. "You did it. You convinced her to give us the next clue."

"Which we just missed 'cause we were busy celebrating," said Emmett, laughing.

The explorers quickly settled down, and Cruz reactivated the journal.

"To find the sixth cipher," said his mother, "journey to the land of the thunder dragon. Follow those who seek the peace found at great height. There, you will be among friends. Say a blessing. Break bread. Walk the path in front of you. Remember, there are no shortcuts to any place worth going. *Tashi delek,* son."

While Cruz's mom was speaking, black brushstrokes began to appear in the air beside her. At first Cruz thought it was an illustration, but he soon realized it was some type of writing. The elegant flow of calligraphy, however, was not the English alphabet.

"It looks like Sanskrit," said Cruz, thinking of the language that originated in ancient India. "I've seen it in Aunt Marisol's books." Once, she'd sent him a postcard in Sanskrit to decode.

By the time the invisible hand finished, six angular symbols hovered above the explorers. They quickly snapped photos. "I think the symbols stand for different sounds," Cruz explained. "See those tiny triangles placed after the first, second, and fourth symbols? I'm pretty sure those are spaces, but I don't know if they're between syllables or words."

Sailor tipped her head. "That one looks like a bird."

Cruz glanced at the V-like stroke perched on the second symbol. It *did* resemble a bird. It was funny how your brain found the familiar among the unfamiliar. He also saw a dangling five and an eight tipped on its side, but, again, he knew they had to be part of the writing.

"Bhutan!" Lani was clutching her tablet. "That's where we have to go! Listen to this: 'The country of Bhutan is known as the land of the thunder dragon because of the powerful thunderstorms that roll into the deep valleys from the high Himalaya.' And look what's on the national flag." She turned her screen to show them a white dragon holding jewels in its talons. The dragon was set on a square background made up of two triangles: one orange, the other yellow. "The dragon is called a *druk*."

Cruz pulled up a map of Bhutan on his own tablet. It was a small country between India and China on the eastern edge of the Himalayan mountains. "It's less than a thousand miles from here."

"The clue said something about great heights," said Emmett. "The tallest peak in Bhutan is Gangkhar Puensum, elevation twenty-four thousand eight hundred thirty-six feet! No one has ever climbed it." He shot Cruz a worried look. "You don't think your mother wants you to hike up *that*, do you?"

"Could be." Cruz winked at Lani and Sailor. "She *did* love mountain climbing."

"Sounds like fun," said Lani, playing along.

"We are explorers, after all." Sailor grinned. "We could be the first people ever to summit it. How cool would that be?"

The color was draining from Emmett's face almost as fast as it was from his emoto-glasses.

Cruz, Lani, and Sailor broke up laughing. Once he realized they were kidding, Emmett relaxed, though it took a while for the pink to return to his cheeks.

"The calligraphy in the clue is probably Bhutanese," concluded Cruz.

After a little research, they discovered the Bhutanese language was also known as Dzongkha. Lani found a chart of the Dzongkha alphabet and they began comparing it to Cruz's photo of the clue. Right away, they ran into trouble. Cruz found Sailor's bird easily enough, however, on the chart it was sitting on a totally different symbol. "See, what we think is one sound could actually be several connected together," said Lani. "Look here: The third symbol is actually two sounds linked together, *ta* and *sa*. But which one comes first?"

"The thingy that looks like a number five is on the bottom. I bet it's *sa-ta*," said Cruz.

"Could be, but even if you're right, we don't speak the language," said Emmett. "We need someone to translate it."

"We'll have to do it once we get to Bhutan," said Cruz. "Speaking of that, it's getting late. I'd better contact Aunt Marisol." He sent an urgent message to her, saying they needed Captain Roxas to fly them to Bhutan as soon as possible. When his tablet started to chime a minute later, he assumed it was his aunt.

Cruz tapped his screen, but the woman that appeared was not the one he expected to see. "Uh . . . Dr. Hightower?"

That got everyone's attention. Three heads popped up to look at Cruz.

"Good evening, Cruz." The Academy president's cream turtleneck stood out against the black headrest of the throne chair in her office. "Actually, it's lunchtime here." She dipped a metal spoon into a white porcelain bowl covered with little purple violets. "Water chestnut and dumpling soup is perfect on a cold winter's day. Your aunt told me you were on your way to India to find the next piece of the cipher. I know it's late, but I wanted to check in."

"Everything's great," replied Cruz. "We found the fifth cipher."

"Excellent."

"We also solved part of Mom's next clue. The sixth cipher is in Bhutan."

"Bhutan?" She delicately sipped her soup. "Yes, well . . . let's discuss it."

Wuh-oh. Usually when his dad said that, it meant Cruz wasn't going to get to do something he wanted to do. Or if he *did* get to do it, some strict rules were imposed.

Dr. Hightower's spiked white hair, which reminded Cruz of the top of a lemon meringue pie, loomed close to the camera. "I'm assuming this trip means you will not be in class on Monday morning."

Cruz gave a slight shake of his head.

"Or Tuesday, or perhaps even Wednesday?"

He dropped his eyes. "Probably not," he muttered.

"You know that I admire and support your quest to fulfill your mother's mission," said Dr. Hightower. "But I am beginning to wonder if you aren't biting off more than you can chew."

"I … I'm not," stuttered Cruz. "I always complete any assignments I miss. Ask any of my professors. I'm getting good grades—"

"I'm well aware of your grades. My point is that you can't hear a lecture if you're not in the room. And may I remind you that you are not the only one involved here, Cruz. You'll note that three more of my freshman explorers are also not where they're supposed to be."

Looking at his friends, Cruz's shoulders sagged. He didn't know what to say. He couldn't argue with Dr. Hightower. During Cruz's conversation with the Academy president, his friends had gathered in front of him. Silent messages began to pass between them.

She's not going to let us go to Bhutan, flashed Emmett's bright orange and mushroom brown glasses.

What do we do? asked Sailor's raised eyebrows.

Think, think, THINK! cried Lani's wringing hands.

Dr. Hightower looked like a stern judge about to render her verdict. Cruz felt helpless. If she ordered them back to *Orion,* they would have to go.

"Tell her about Mr. Rook," spit Sailor.

Dr. Hightower's spoon clattered into the bowl. Flecks of water chestnut and dumpling soup hit the camera lens. "Did you say Rook?"

"Yes," said Emmett. "Mr. Rook is trying to find the next piece of the cipher before we do."

Furrows plowed across Dr. Hightower's forehead. "How do you know this?"

"A . . . a reliable source," said Cruz.

"But he can't possibly know where you're headed next. Only a few of us do, and we keep it a guarded secret."

The explorers exchanged looks. Who was going to tell her?

"It might not be as much of a secret as we thought." Cruz winced. "We . . . uh . . . found out that Nebula has spies . . . a couple of them may be on board *Orion*."

"That's why we can't go back to the ship," said Sailor. "Not yet. Mr. Rook only needs to get one piece of the cipher to make sure we never complete it."

"Please let us go to Bhutan," begged Cruz. "I promise I'll get back to *Orion* as quickly as I can. And if you want Emmett, Lani, and Sailor to return now, I'll go alone—"

"No!" cried his friends. Lani, Sailor, and Emmett folded their arms in defiance.

Dr. Hightower leaned back in her chair and tapped her fingertips together. "I suppose we could arrange to tape the lectures so you wouldn't miss your classes, although you still wouldn't be there actively participating . . . But it's only for a few days and you aren't *that* far from your next destination . . . Still, allowing you to miss school puts a chink in the cornerstone of the high expectations we set for all of our students . . ."

The explorers stayed perfectly still as she debated it.

Finally, Dr. Hightower brought her hand down against the desk with a loud thump. "Okay. You may go to Bhutan."

"All of us?" asked Cruz.

"All of you."

Cruz bumped fists with Emmett and Lani.

"But . . ."

Cruz stiffened. For such a tiny word, it could bring a whole lot of trouble.

"Due to the dangerous and unpredictable nature of Mr. Malcolm Rook, I want an adult to accompany you on your journey."

A chaperone? Emmett was making a sour face. Sailor was chomping on her lower lip. Cruz felt the same way, but he knew Dr. Hightower. This wasn't a request.

"I will assign someone to accompany you," said Dr. Hightower. "Also, you must be back on *Orion* by curfew Wednesday night. No later. Those are my terms. Do you accept?"

"We do," said Cruz without hesitation.

"Going by helicopter will take too long," said Dr. Hightower. "You'll take *Condor*."

Sweet! She was sending the Academy's plane for them.

"Thank you, Dr. Hightower," said Cruz.

"Please do be careful. I want you all back safe and sound. I'll brief your aunt and Taryn on the situation."

Taryn!

Cruz had totally forgotten about her. It was already after ten o'clock. The second he hung up with Dr. Hightower, Cruz sent Taryn a message: *Sorry I'm late. Meant to call. We're okay!*

She texted back immediately: *Thanks for touching base. Get some sleep. Gotta go. Dr. Hightower is calling. Good night.*

Sailor, Emmett, and Lani, said their good nights, too, and headed off to their rooms.

After the day he'd had, Cruz should have been out two seconds after his head touched the pillow. Instead, tucked under the pink lotus quilt, he found himself wide awake and staring at a white ceiling trimmed in gold molding. It felt strange, not having Emmett here. Weird, huh? He'd spent 12 years sleeping in a room by himself, but now, after four and half months at the Academy, he couldn't imagine not having a roommate. Things sure could change quickly.

He wondered who Dr. Hightower would send with them to Bhutan. Wouldn't it be great if it was Aunt Marisol? Not likely. She had classes to teach. It would probably be one of the security officers. If so, they weren't out of the woods. Officer Wardicorn had turned out to be working for Nebula, which mean it was possible that someone on the security team was Zebra.

Zebra.

Who was he? Or she? That mystery would have to wait. For now, Cruz needed to focus on finding the sixth cipher. He was grateful to Dr. Hightower. In spite of everything, the Academy president had put her faith in him.

So had his mom.

Cruz was not about to let either one of them down.

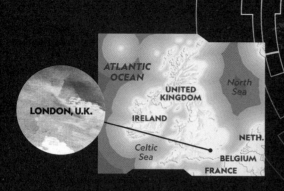

18

THORNE PRESCOTT *trotted down the steps of the last eggshell white town house in a row of identical town houses. The morning rain misted his cheek as he strolled to where a black car idled at the curb. Tossing his bag into the back seat, Prescott got into the front passenger seat and buckled in. The two men did not greet each other.*

Behind the wheel, Malcolm Rook signaled, then pulled out into London traffic.

Ever the chameleon, Rook had altered his appearance again. He'd chopped off most of his hair and shaved his beard. He'd colored his hair, too, but something had gone wrong. He looked like an orange Popsicle.

Prescott took his mirrored pilot's sunglasses from the front pocket of his jacket and slid them on. There wasn't a ray of sun in sight.

Rook gave him a sideways glance. "Don't you want to know where we're going?"

"I know," answered Prescott flatly. "So does Lion."

"What? How in the—"

"This is Hezekiah Brume we're talking about." It felt good to say it out loud. No code names. "Brume knows what color socks you're wearing."

"Shows what he knows. I'm not wearing socks." Rook glanced in the rearview mirror. "You're supposed to throw him off our trail."

"I'm not the only one working for him." Prescott stretched out his long legs. "And I don't answer to you, Rook. We're partners—or did you forget that?"

"I'll hold up my end of the deal. I'm not on some power trip. I only want what's fair, what I was promised when this whole thing started. I'm not like him. Or you."

Hardly. As far as Prescott could tell, Rook was exactly like Brume. Prescott didn't know Cruz Coronado. But Rook certainly did. There had been a teacher-student connection between the two. Friendship. Trust. Yet, Rook appeared to feel no guilt about betraying that bond. Plus, if it weren't for Cruz, Rook would be a pancake on the floor of the Academy's library. Did any of it make Rook feel compassion for the kid? Was there a smidge of loyalty? An ounce of gratitude?

Nope. Prescott saw nothing but selfishness. The greedy have no shame.

Not that Prescott was much better. Rook was right. He had done awful things. But Prescott didn't pretend anyone owed him anything. The word "fair" wasn't in his vocabulary.

Rook was still checking his rearview mirror. That could mean only one thing. Prescott glanced in his rain-splattered side mirror. "Looks like we have company."

"I . . . I think so." Rook sounded nervous.

Prescott wasn't surprised. Cowards are always brave until the first test.

Gripping the wheel tighter, Rook pressed on the gas. "I'll lose them."

"Pull over," ordered Prescott.

"Are you crazy? I can't—"

"Pull over."

Rook swung into a spot at the curb in front of a pet food store. The window was jammed with stuffed poodles wearing snowflake sweaters.

Prescott flung open his door. He hopped out, opened the back door, and reached for his bag. "I'll meet you at the airport."

Rook leaned over the passenger seat. "But—"

Prescott slammed the door. He started walking. He did not look back until he reached the corner. Rook was driving away, a silver SUV tailing him.

Two blocks later, once he was sure he wasn't being followed, Prescott turned down an alley. He'd catch a cab at the corner of Ladbroke and Holland Park. Something in the back window of Chaucer's Book Shoppe caught his eye. Among the puppets and books and toys of a cluttered children's section sat a young woman, a curly-headed toddler in denim overalls in her lap. They were reading a big picture book with bunnies on the cover; the mother bent so far forward her cheek was brushing her daughter's. The little girl stretched out her fingers to touch the turning pages, as if she didn't want the story to end. He let himself grin. Piper used to reach for the pages, too.

A honking horn snapped Prescott back to reality. He went on his way. At the intersection, he hailed a taxi and jumped in. "Heathrow Airport," he directed the driver.

Prescott had a text. It was from Komodo.

It may be January, but it's May Day.

Komodo had done it. Events were in motion now that nobody, not even Rook, could stop.

It was getting tricky, walking this tightrope. Prescott had often wondered who he would side with in the end: Rook or Brume? Now it looked like he wouldn't have to choose.

If the surprise Brume had in store for Cruz worked out, the game would be over before the day was.

19

▶ **"YOU HAVE ARRIVED** at your destination," said the car's dashboard computer. "The current air temperature at Kheria Airport is seventy-four degrees and the time is one nineteen p.m. Thank you for choosing Auto Auto."

Cruz, Emmett, Sailor, and Lani piled out of the vehicle, grabbed their duffels and packs, and headed into the airport. The terminal was small, yet clean and modern with steel beams and tall glass windows. Once through security, they went past a convenience store, a newsstand, and a café that overlooked the end of the runway. Taryn's text had said *Condor* would be landing around two o'clock, so they had a little time.

"Anybody hungry?" asked Emmett. He looked at the puzzled faces surrounding him. "What? It's almost dinnertime."

"In *four* hours," snorted Sailor.

"We have to wait somewhere."

They headed for the café.

The explorers shared a plate of *pani puri,* an appetizer their server recommended. Cruz took one of the deep-fried balls of dough that looked like doughnut holes. He bit into the crunchy pastry, releasing a warm filling of potatoes and chutney. It was good; sweet yet tangy!

"Pani puri is puri heaven!" said Sailor, popping another of the puffs into her mouth. "I could eat these all day."

"Good thing you're not hungry," clipped Emmett.

They also ordered rice and korma, chicken cooked in a sauce of almond curry, tomato paste, cream, and spices like ginger, cardamom, and paprika. The smell alone made Cruz's stomach gurgle. Everything was delicious!

Wiping his mouth, Cruz saw the flicker of lights in the milky afternoon sky. The black jet continued its smooth approach, cruising in to make a perfect landing in front of them. Seeing *EA* in giant gold letters next to the school's logo on the side of the plane always gave Cruz goose bumps. *Condor* was taxiing across the tarmac. It was headed toward the first gate at the opposite end of the terminal.

"Come on!" said Cruz, tossing his napkin onto the table.

They paid for their meal, grabbed their gear, and took off.

"Wait for me," cried Sailor. She had stopped to snag the last three pani puri, stuffing them into her pocket. "I'm not leaving without these!"

Emmett turned to Cruz as they hurried through the airport. "We're going to Paro, right?"

"Yep. It's the only international airport in Bhutan." Paro was in the western part of the country. Cruz prayed it was close to where the clue

would be directing them. He'd read that Bhutan was a nation of extremes—dense forests, deep gorges, soaring peaks.

"Did you know it's one of the most difficult airports to land a plane?" panted Emmett.

"Because of the mountains?"

"Only a handful of pilots in the world are allowed to land there."

"Let's hope Captain Wada is one of them."

"Let's hope!"

"Taryn," said Lani, passing between the boys.

Cruz gave her a funny look. "Taryn's a pilot?"

Lani pointed. "*Taryn.*"

Cruz stopped short. Calmly strolling toward them, wearing an olive green jacket with pink fleece trim, black pants, and hiking boots, was Taryn Secliff!

Cruz felt the strap of his duffel fall from his shoulder.

When Dr. Hightower had required that someone go with them, he hadn't counted on that person being Taryn. Not that Cruz was upset. Far from it. If he could choose anyone on *Orion* other than Aunt Marisol to come along, Taryn would be right up there in the top two (Fanchon being the other).

"Hello!" Their adviser seemed to enjoy seeing the looks of surprise on their faces. She gave them each a quick squeeze. "Ground rules. I'm going with you to Paro and beyond, if necessary, for the next three and a half days. I ask no questions. I need no explanations. I do, however, insist upon one thing: No one leaves my sight. Got it?"

They did.

Taryn reached for Cruz's duffel and put the strap back over his shoulder. "Your magic carpet awaits."

"What about Hubbard?" asked Cruz, finally finding his voice.

"Fanchon's looking after him." She snickered. "Along with twenty helpers, aka your classmates. I think my dog has playdates lined up for the next month."

In single file, Lani, Sailor, Emmett, Cruz, and Taryn climbed the steps to the jet. They were welcomed at the door by Mr. Neering and Ms. Bukhari, *Condor*'s flight attendants. As they began to make their way into the fuselage to choose their seats, a door opened behind them. Captain Wada and First Officer Ionescu came out of the cockpit.

"Welcome, explorers!" Captain Wada was putting on her blazer. She flipped her hair over the collar. "We need to fuel up—both the aircraft and ourselves—but then we'll be on our way."

Cruz nudged Emmett. "You gonna ask?"

"Uh…um…" His emoto-glasses were morphing into light blue circles of embarrassment.

Captain Wada tipped her head. "Something on your mind?"

Sailor, who was ahead of Emmett, flung her bag into an overhead bin. "He read that it's super mega dangerous to land at Paro."

"I wouldn't say super mega dangerous," said Captain Wada with a grin. "Challenging, perhaps, but—"

"Is it true that only a handful of pilots are allowed to do it?" asked Lani.

"Yes, that is correct—"

"Then we're breaking the rules?" said Sailor, taking a window seat.

"You can all rest easy," said First Officer Ionescu. "Captain Wada is one of those well-qualified and very capable pilots that is certified to land at Paro. She's done it many times. As have I. Not to worry, explorers. You're in good hands."

"I…I knew that," said Emmett, quickly sliding in next to Sailor.

Lani took the row opposite Emmett and Sailor. She wanted to stretch out and nap, so Cruz moved to the row behind her. He scooted to the window seat. Taryn sat beside him.

As usual, Cruz spent takeoff with his nose glued to the window so he could see everything. The plane lifted off to the southwest over the farmlands and then banked, giving them a sweeping view of the city—the tightly packed buildings, the gray stretches of highway, the muddy green ribbon of the Yamuna River.

"There's the Taj Mahal!" said Sailor.

As they flew over the onion-shaped domes and spires of the grand tomb, Taryn leaned over Cruz for a look. "Oh, isn't that a beautiful sight? I've always wanted to visit."

His pulse quickened. "Uh ... same here."

"Good afternoon from the flight deck." Captain Wada's voice came through the speakers. "Looks like we have fairly smooth sailing to Paro. We're going to skirt south a bit to avoid a storm. Flight time is about one hour and thirty-five minutes. We're crossing time zones, as well. Bhutan is a half hour ahead of India standard time, so allowing for the time difference, we should be touching down at Paro around five p.m. Sit back, relax, and please let myself, First Officer Ionescu, or Mr. Neering and Ms. Bukhari know if there's anything we can do to make your trip more enjoyable."

Cruz didn't feel like watching a movie. He was caught up on his homework, though that would certainly change tomorrow. Eating was definitely out. Cruz was stuffed to his eyeballs with pani puri and korma. Reading? That sounded good. He took out his tablet and did some research on where they were headed. The Paro valley was at an elevation of 7,200 feet. Daytime temperatures in January were in the low 50s, but then dropped to below freezing overnight. Depending on how high they had to trek, it could get much colder. Cruz was glad he'd brought his hide-and-seek jacket. He'd almost left it behind on *Orion*.

Beside him, Taryn had taken out her crochet bag. She'd plopped a big ball of variegated yarn in her lap. The colors went from gold to light green to dark green to deep brown then back to gold again, repeating over and over on the same string. She was pushing a blue crochet hook in and out of the yarn, moving so quickly, her red fingernails were a blur. He watched the strand of yarn pass through her fingers and join the pattern to become a row of stitches that looked like miniature fans.

"I like the colors," said Cruz.

"It's called Firefly Summer."

"It reminds me of Emmett's glasses when he's working on an invention," he noted.

"It does." She chuckled. "The ombré yarns create their own pattern depending on the stitch you use, so no two pieces are ever quite the same."

"What are you making?"

"You'll laugh."

"I won't."

"A sweater for Hubbard."

He laughed. "Sorry."

"I know," she sighed. "Ordinarily, Hubbard would not stand for being dressed up, but this is for practical reasons. It gets chilly in his meadow and he's been shivering. I thought he could wear it under his life preserver to keep warm."

"It's a good idea," said Cruz.

She sure loved her dog.

"Taryn?"

"Hmmm?"

"I just wanted to say ... I mean, this trip ... going to Bhutan and everything ..."

"I told you, you don't have to explain."

"Yes, but ... I *will* tell you more when I can ..." Cruz knew he wasn't making sense, but how do you tell someone you want so badly to trust that you want so badly to trust them?

The hook stopped. Taryn turned to him. "I know all I need to know," she said softly. "There isn't anything I wouldn't do to keep my explorers safe. And that's all *you* need to know."

He let his head fall back against the seat. Cruz watched her crochet, his eyelids getting heavier and heavier...

"Good evening." Captain Wada's calm voice woke him. "We'll be making our descent into Paro International Airport shortly."

That was quick!

Stretching, Cruz gazed out at the craggy white peaks of the high Himalaya. He thought of the Mount Everest–themed dorm room he shared with Emmett back at the Academy. A TV screen on their wall carried a 24/7 live cam stream from one of the base camps. Cruz would often watch it when he needed a break from his homework or couldn't sleep or just because it was there. He'd wonder where the climbers were from and what they were thinking. Were they excited? Terrified? Most people survived the treacherous ascent, but not everyone. Several hundred people had died on Everest. Cruz and Emmett had looked it up. Whenever he saw people begin their trek toward the summit, Cruz would touch one of the prayer flags that decorated his room and wish them good luck. Now he was here in a part of the world he'd viewed every day for weeks. Was it his turn to scale a mountain? Would anyone wish him good luck?

The plane lurched.

Lani's head appeared around her seat, her eyes wide. She'd only been on a jet a few times. Cruz knew the ride to Turkey to join the Academy was her longest plane trip ever.

"Just turbulence," soothed Cruz. "You know, like ocean waves back home but over the mountains."

"We'll be on the ground soon enough," said Taryn.

Lani stuck out her tongue. "That's what I'm worried about."

A moment later, *Condor* jerked again. The ball of yarn rolled out of Taryn's lap.

Cruz checked his seat belt. "You okay, Lani? There might be a few more bumps bef—"

Suddenly, *Condor* rolled sharply to the left. Cruz's shoulder smashed into the fuselage wall. He heard the overhead bins popping open. Out the window, Cruz saw the green and white of snow-tipped trees coming up to meet them. The plane was going into a steep dive!

"Everyone, heads down!" shouted Taryn. "Emmett, take off your glasses."

"Brace yourselves!" called Mr. Neering. He'd buckled himself into a seat across the aisle from Cruz and Taryn.

Cruz bent forward, tucked his head, and hugged his knees the way the flight attendants had instructed before takeoff. His hands and feet were tingling. His chest felt like it was going to burst. This couldn't be happening! He didn't even have a minute to call his dad and say good-bye. Seconds. That's what he had. Seconds.

"Brace! Brace!" shouted both Mr. Neering and Ms. Bukhari, from somewhere behind him. They repeated it again and again.

Blindly flinging out a hand, he found Taryn's knee, then her fist. Her palm turned and she grabbed on. She held on so tightly he thought the bones in his fingers would shatter.

Everything was screaming in his ears— thundering engines and frantic voices and his own pummeling heart. The noise was deafening, but Cruz didn't care because it meant he was still alive. For one more second, he was still on Earth.

Soon enough, he knew, there would be silence.

"Brace! Brace!"

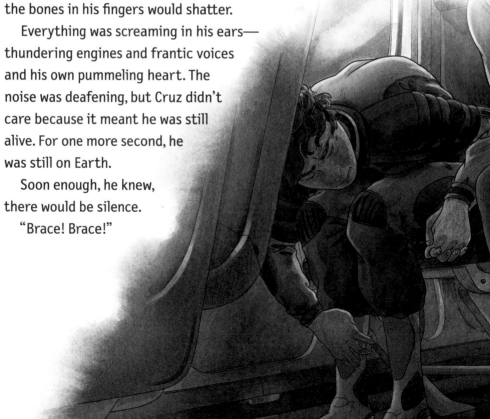

20

"CRUZ?"

The roaring tornado was gone. He heard no shrill voices, only the even hum of jet engines. Wrapped in a tight ball, Cruz lifted his head.

"We've leveled out." Taryn's voice was hoarse. "I think we're all right now."

Uncoiling himself, Cruz put a shaky hand between the seat and the window. "Lani?"

A cold finger latched on to his pinkie. "I . . . I'm here. That was some mountain wave."

"Sure was," he whispered, although they both knew enough about air currents to realize that turbulence wasn't to blame for what had happened.

Condor banked and they began to dip between the peaks. Cruz watched the rolling hills, covered in pines, flatten out to the terraced farmlands of the valley. He watched the wing flaps adjust and heard the whir of landing gear being lowered. After a few more turns, *Condor* was bumping down the runway. They had made it!

The plane came to a stop at the gate, yet no one moved.

The cockpit door opened and Captain Wada appeared. "Is anyone injured?"

Everyone seemed to be okay.

"What happened?" asked Emmett.

"A computer malfunction, as far as we can tell," said the first officer. "We'll be thoroughly investigating."

"We'll leave you to your work," said Taryn, unbuckling her seat belt. "Explorers?"

They quickly collected their gear and made their way down the aisle.

Cruz's legs felt rubbery in the plane but firmed up once his soles hit the asphalt on the tarmac. The sun had already slipped behind the hills, leaving the sky a soft bluish purple. Someone said something about it being freezing, but Cruz wasn't cold. The wind felt good. And it felt even better to be alive.

The three-story terminal had a templelike look with a flat roofline that extended beyond the walls. Rows of small windows were trimmed in dark wood. Inside, intricate and colorful paintings decorated the terminal. A mural of a Buddhist dharma wheel symbol between two orange-and-red serpents flowed across an archway. Red, blue, and yellow chevrons stretched across the tops of walls. An endless knot pattern wrapped around balcony railings and posts. They headed across the cream-colored marble floor to a corner of empty chairs.

"Taryn, can you give us a minute?" asked Cruz. He didn't want to hurt her feelings, but he needed to discuss the next step with the team.

"I'll get some coffee." She nodded to a little stand across the terminal.

Once she'd left, they huddled up. "Do you think what happened on *Condor* was an accident?" asked Sailor.

"Unlikely," said Emmett, cleaning his glasses. "The chances of you being in a plane crash are, like, one in eleven million. A plane doesn't suddenly go into a dive."

"Unless someone wants it to," said Lani.

Cruz knew they were all thinking the same thing: Nebula.

"How do they do that?" fumed Sailor. "Cruz told Felipe he was going to Madagascar. That should have thrown Nebula off our trail."

"And we didn't even know we were going to Bhutan until yesterday," said Lani.

"Maybe they have more spies than we thought," said Emmett.

"Crikey!" exclaimed Sailor. "How many do you think—"

"Let's not freak out," cautioned Cruz. "We can't worry about what Nebula knows and doesn't know. Let's stay focused and stick to the plan. We'll rent our Auto Auto and head to the hotel Taryn booked. In the morning, we'll find the library and have someone translate the Dzongkha message."

"I bet the hotel clerk could do it," said Sailor.

Lani shook her head. "Maybe, but if someone is following us, we'll be making it too easy for them to find out what we know."

"Good point," agreed Sailor. "We'll go to the library. I just hope it isn't giving Mr. Rook and Prescott time to catch up to us."

"As long as we keep moving, we should be fine," said Cruz.

"I wouldn't be so sure about that," whispered Emmett.

Cruz wiped his bleary eyes. "Why not?"

"Because right now our adviser is talking to the enemy."

"*What?*"

"At the coffee shop." Emmett's glasses had turned a fearful white. "Don't turn—"

Cruz whirled around. Taryn was standing near the counter, waiting for her coffee and chatting with a handsome man in snakeskin-print cowboy boots. Prescott!

"Can we freak out *now*?" rasped Sailor.

"Freak out and get out," said Cruz. "We need to get Taryn away from him, for her safety and ours."

"I'll do it," broke in Lani. "Prescott doesn't know me. I'll get her and we'll meet you at the hotel."

Cruz frowned. "I don't know, Lani—"

"Are you going to stand here and argue with me *now*?"

When she took that tone, Cruz knew better than to go toe to toe with her. "Okay."

Throwing his duffel over one shoulder and his backpack over the other, Cruz slipped into the aisle closest to the wall. Emmett and Sailor

were right behind him. The trio crept along, slipping from one post to the next until they made it to the Autonomous Auto kiosk near the terminal entrance.

Soon, they were stuffing their gear in the trunk of a tiny copper-colored car. Sailor and Cruz got in the front. Emmett hopped in back.

"*Joen pa Leg So*," said the soft-voiced onboard computer.

"English, please!" ordered Sailor.

"Welcome to Auto Auto. Please input your—"

"Yeah, yeah, yeah, just GO!" barked Cruz, glancing back at the terminal door.

"I'm sorry," said the monotone voice. "In order to accommodate you, I will need a destination. If you have a partial address, cross street, or business name, I can help determine your location. If you aren't sure where you want to go, tell me what type of service you require. I can give you options and even make a reservation for you—"

"One second," said Cruz. Taryn had sent him the name of the hotel but it was on his tablet, which, naturally, was in his backpack in the trunk. He looked from Sailor to Emmett. "Do any of you know which hotel we're going to?"

They shook their heads.

Cruz flung open his door. "Auto Auto, open the trunk, please."

"Cruz!" called Sailor. "That greeting. The Auto Auto speaks Dzongkha."

Their eyes locked. She was right! The clue!

Cruz leaned toward the dash. "Auto Auto, can you *read* Dzongkha?"

"Yes," answered the computer. "I am equipped to translate four thousand five hundred twenty-seven written and spoken languages, Bhutanese, also called Dzongkha, being one of them."

Jumping out of the car, Cruz ran around to the trunk, grabbed his tablet from his backpack, and rushed back—all in less than 10 seconds. Cruz turned on his tablet and pulled up the photo of the calligraphy in his mother's clue. He aimed it at the camera on the dash. "What does this say?" he huffed.

"Your text reads: 'Paro Taktsang.'"

"What does it mean?"

"Paro Taktsang, or the Tiger's Nest, is a sacred Buddhist monastery and caves located on a mountainside overlooking the upper Paro valley."

Sailor bounced. "We're in the Paro valley. Aren't we?"

"That's correct," said Auto Auto.

Cruz's pulse quickened. "How far is the Tiger's Nest from here?"

"The trailhead to the Tiger's Nest is approximately eleven point three miles from your present location," answered the computer. "Travel time is estimated at thirty-four minutes. However, the temple is now closed. It will reopen tomorrow morning at—"

Bomp, bomp!

Someone was banging on the back passenger-side door! It was Lani. Taryn was with her. Their adviser was scowling.

Emmett threw open the back door. "I don't see Prescott."

Lani jumped in and scooted to the middle.

Taryn bent. "What's going on? Why did you—"

"Get in!" shouted Cruz.

Taryn slid in and slammed the door.

"Auto Auto, book us into a hotel near the Tiger's Nest that has three rooms available for tonight and take us there," said Cruz. He glanced back at the terminal. "Now, please!"

"Reservation made and destination acknowledged for Paro Chu Inn." The car started up. They rolled out of the airport parking lot with Cruz's eyes glued to the rearview. Sailor and Lani were watching the side mirrors. Once they'd put several miles behind them and Cruz was sure Prescott wasn't following them, he turned in his seat. "Sorry, Taryn."

Her face was pinched. "Ground rules, remember?"

"It wasn't Cruz's fault," said Sailor. "It was that man ..."

"What man?" asked Taryn.

A wave of panic swept through Cruz as a thought struck—a

head-pounding, gut-flipping, heart-ripping thought. Taryn was the spy! She was Zebra!

Sailor turned to peer around her seat. "The one you were talking to at the coffee shop. See, he—" Before she could finish, Cruz grabbed Sailor's arm. He shook his head.

Don't do it. Don't tell her.

"What about him?" pressed Taryn.

"Uh . . . he was the . . . reason we left?" Sailor frowned at Cruz. "We . . . um . . . didn't want to be rude and interrupt your conversation, so . . . uh . . . we thought we'd get the car while Lani waited for you?"

"Next time, interrupt me." Taryn's tone was curt. "Look, I know you're all used to doing your own thing on these missions, but Dr. Hightower's instructions were clear. You don't have to tell me what you're doing or why, but you cannot do it alone, do you understand? No splitting up without my say-so, even to get the car . . ." Her lecture lasted nearly the whole way to the hotel.

The more Taryn scolded them, the more Cruz realized how silly he'd been to think that she was working for Nebula. If his adviser was the spy, she certainly wouldn't have met with Prescott in a public terminal with the explorers 30 feet away.

Once Cruz had settled into the room he was sharing with Emmett on the third floor of Paro Chu Inn, he got on his tablet. He needed to know more about Tiger's Nest. Cruz logged on to the Bhutan National Archives site. He learned that in the 17th century, a monastery was built around a cave in the high cliffs where a Buddhist master had med-itated centuries before. According to legend, the master flew to the cave on the back of a tiger, which is how the temple got its name. Cruz read that the parking lot of the Tiger's Nest was about a half mile from the hotel, but the hike up to the actual temple would take a couple of hours. Cruz messaged Sailor, Lani, and Taryn to let them know they'd need to get an early start in the morning.

There was nothing to do now but wait. Still, Cruz couldn't relax, couldn't stop turning everything over in his mind. Roewyn had said

Mr. Rook and Prescott could be teaming up against her father to get the next cipher piece. If Prescott was here, that meant Mr. Rook was probably with him. And knowing Nebula, there could be more spies out there. Cruz was feeling less and less confident that he could hold them all off.

Cruz wanted to call his dad but there was a 16-hour time difference between Bhutan and Kauai. It was four in the morning back home. He glanced up from his tablet. Emmett was already conked out. Splayed facedown on top of the bed, he hadn't bothered to change into his pajamas. Cruz stared at the video call on his screen. His dad *had* said he could call *any*time…

He pressed the button.

It took his father a few rings to answer. "Cruz?" He was groggy.

"Sorry to wake you," he said quietly, so he wouldn't wake Emmett, too.

"Don't be." His dad rubbed the sleep from his eyes. "Are you still in India?"

"Bhutan. We got the fifth cipher. It was at the Taj Mahal. I'm pretty sure the sixth cipher is at the Tiger's Nest."

"The temple? Knowing your mom, that makes sense. Good work, son."

"I couldn't do this alone, that's for sure. By the way, Taryn's here."

"What?" His dad was awake now!

Hearing Cruz's explanation of Dr. Hightower's terms for their travel, his father chuckled. "You're gaining quite the entourage, aren't you?"

"That's what scares me."

"I see what you mean. You're a bigger target for Nebula."

"And now Mr. Rook." He told his dad about Roewyn and her warning.

"Rook does complicate things," said his dad, rubbing his chin. "But Dr. Hightower is right. Stick together. Stay close to Taryn. There's safety in numbers."

"I will." That did make him feel better. "I'll call you later, hopefully, after we get the sixth cipher."

"Watch your step."

"I will. Good night—I mean, good morning."

"Night, son. I love you."

"Love you, too."

After hanging up, Cruz nudged Emmett. His roommate rolled off the mattress, zombie-walked to put his pajamas on, and crawled under the covers. Cruz brushed his teeth and was about to put his pj's on, too, when he heard a soft knock at the door.

"Who is it?"

"Lani."

Cruz opened up.

"I have to talk to you," she whispered, stepping in.

Cruz shut the door. He could tell by her face something was wrong. "What is it?"

"The man at the airport—Prescott? I've seen him before."

The hair on the back of Cruz's neck stood up.

"He was at the observatory on Mauna Kea when the police were arresting the kidnappers," explained Lani. "I remember it because most people, when they see police cars, are curious. They want to see what's going on. Not him. He drove by without even so much as turning his head. But I got a good look at his face, and that was him at the airport today. No doubt." She bit her lip. "He's one of your dad's kidnappers, isn't he?"

Lani had confirmed what he'd long suspected.

"Yes," answered Cruz.

"Should we turn him in?"

"We can't call the police now. It'll draw too much attention to us. The best we can do is go to the Tiger's Nest, get the sixth cipher, and get out of here as fast as we can." Cruz ran his hands through his hair. "We've got to protect each other. And Taryn. Especially Taryn. We know what he's capable of. She doesn't. She doesn't even know why we're here." Dr. Hightower had thought she was helping him by sending their adviser, but it had only made things more complicated. It was one more person he had to be responsible for.

"You look beat. We can talk more on the hike up to the Tiger's Nest in the morning." Lani opened the door. "Get some sleep. Good night."

"Night, *hoaaloha*." Cruz shut the door behind her.

Prescott had to be some kind of wizard to find out where they were going *and* get there ahead of them! And was Roewyn right? Had he really teamed up with Mr. Rook? And if so, where was the devious librarian? Cruz was worried, and not only about keeping Taryn out of harm's way. If anything ever happened to Emmett, Sailor, or Lani...

He was beginning to wonder if his dad had been wrong. What if there wasn't safety in numbers? What if there was only more danger? There was only one way he could think of to protect everyone.

Grabbing a pen, Cruz scribbled a note on the pad on the nightstand between his bed and Emmett's. His roommate began to stir. Cruz froze. Emmett mumbled something in his sleep, then turned over. Cruz gently set down the pen. Pulling his hide-and-seek jacket out of his duffel, Cruz scooped up his backpack and shoes and tiptoed out the door.

Maybe the safest number of all was one.

21

►**CRUZ'S** breath came in quick frosty clouds. His hide-and-seek jacket kept his core warm but his hands and toes were icicles. After slipping some money under the ticket booth door and hopping the split rail gate, he started up the trail to the Tiger's Nest.

The path was not lit, but it was a clear night. Between the nearly full moon, the bioluminescent side of his reversible jacket, Mell's glowing eyes, and his OS band, Cruz had enough illumination to see a good 10 to 12 feet ahead of him. The banners of red, yellow, green, blue, and white prayer flags that lined the path also helped. Still, it wasn't an easy hike. The trail was narrow, rocky, and incredibly steep.

The rapid change in altitude forced Cruz to stop more than once to catch his breath. He'd learned in Professor Modi's class that the higher you went, the less oxygen was found in the air. Plus, in alpine regions, the air pressure is lower than it is in a person's lungs, so the body has to work harder to pump oxygen through the veins. Cruz's GPS showed he was trekking from a starting elevation of 7,000 feet up to 10,000 feet, and boy were his lungs feeling every foot!

Cruz could almost hear Professor Modi say, "It takes a few days for your body to boost production of red blood cells and adjust to the altitude change."

"Sorry ... Professor," wheezed Cruz, navigating a sharp switchback in the trail. "Don't have ... a few days."

Snap!

Cruz stopped. The noise had come from in front of him.

"Mell," he whispered. "Go check out that sound."

Her lights revealed a row of about a dozen prayer wheels made out of bottles. They were lined up side by side between two posts along the side of the path. Some of the wheels were turning in the wind. That must have been what made the crackling noise.

Taking a swig of water, Cruz took a minute to gaze up at the towering pines. They were so tall, the light could not reach their tops. Cruz put his water bottle away and continued on.

Cruz kept a steady pace but did not rush. He knew that in the darkness a slip on a rock or the turn of an ankle could send him plunging over the side to the ravine below. After nearly two hours of hiking, Cruz reached a flight of thin stone steps that, to his surprise, went down. They kept leading him down, down, down . . .

Could this be right? Had he made a wrong turn?

He heard whooshing. It made him laugh—a laugh that the thin, cold air turned into a cough. Cruz said it out loud, only because Sailor wasn't here to say it: "Not another waterfall!"

Mell was flying ahead, lighting up the gush of water spilling over the top of the cliffs and a thin walking bridge that crossed it. Streamers of prayer flags were everywhere, flapping in the night breeze. Past the bridge, the stairs went up again—hundreds and hundreds of steps. Taking a turn, Cruz saw the silhouette of a building, then a golden tiered roof glittering in the moonlight. Cruz practically ran the last 25 steps to the covered porch of the monastery. He'd made it to the Tiger's Nest!

Cruz stood in the stone alcove, hands on his hips, breathing heavily. He knew he'd have to wait until morning for the temple to open, but that was all right. He would be first inside. It would give him at least a two-hour head start on Prescott, assuming the assassin had discovered where Cruz had gone.

Sliding off his backpack, Cruz set it in the corner near the stone wall, then settled down beside it. Mell's lights were getting dim, signaling her solar-powered battery was running low. Cruz turned off the drone and placed her in his left outer pocket. Flipping up his hood, he drew his legs up to his chest to keep his body heat in. He put his hand into his right pocket, his fingers curling around the octopod. Just in case. Cruz leaned his head against his pack and, finally, closed his eyes for the night.

He listened to the fluttering prayer flags and the cascading water and the sound of his own breath. Cruz repeated his mother's clue so that he would be able to recall it when the time came:

Follow those who seek the peace found at great height. There, you will be among friends. Say a blessing. Break bread. Walk the path in front of you. Remember, there are no shortcuts to any place worth going. Tashi delek, *son.*

Cruz said it once more. Then again.

His eyes were getting heavy.

Follow those who seek the peace . . .

Someone was tapping his shoulder. Cruz jerked back and, forgetting he was against a wall, smacked his head. The octopod still clutched in his right hand, Cruz used his free hand to throw off his hood. He stared up into a halo of light. It encircled the bald head of an elderly monk. The slim figure was wrapped in the folds of dark red robes.

The monk took Cruz's left hand. He turned it over and rubbed it between his own hands to warm it. The monk saw Cruz's pinkish double-helix birthmark. With a finger, he traced the segment not hidden by the Academy's OS band. Cruz saw the time on his band. It was 4:14 a.m.

"I'm Cruz Coronado," he whispered. "I . . . I'm sorry . . . I'm early."

"You are on time," said the monk gently. "Come in." He helped Cruz to his feet.

Cruz lifted his backpack off the ground and followed the monk inside. He was instructed to hang his coat and pack on one of the hooks near the door, and to remove his shoes. Even through his thick socks, the cold stone felt icy under his feet.

The monk led Cruz down a short corridor to a large room with creaky hardwood floors. The room was about the size of the third-floor lounge on *Orion*. It had a small circular skylight but no windows. It was lit by candles, their wicks burning in metal goblets of oil. Each corner held a cluster of a dozen or so of these candle lamps. The only furnishing was a rectangular teak table just inside the door. It was about knee height, as if made for a child.

Cruz looked around. "What should I . . .?" he started, but the elderly man had left.

Minutes later, the monk returned with a tray of food. "First, you must eat." He knelt, placing the food on the little table. Cruz sank down, too. His host bowed his head and, not wanting to be impolite, Cruz did the same. He closed his eyes. Remembering his mom's instructions to offer a blessing, he said a quick prayer of thanks. When Cruz opened his eyes, he was alone.

The tray held a bowl of oatmeal, a thick slice of dark bread, a little package of nuts, a mug of frothy hot chocolate, and two ceramic cups: one filled with peanut butter and the other with honey. Cruz wasn't hungry, but the clue had directed him to say a blessing *and* break bread. Cruz drizzled some honey on the oatmeal and then tried the cereal, enjoying its sweet, thick warmth. Using the small knife, he spread peanut butter on the soft bread. Okay, maybe he was a *little* hungry. As Cruz reached for the earthen mug of hot chocolate, his hand brushed the package of nuts. A thin red ribbon was tied in a double bow. He'd already had peanut butter. Why had the monk brought nuts, too?

Cruz leaned in. Almonds!

His mother's box! It too contained a small pack of almonds, also tied with a red ribbon in a double bow. Cruz yanked on the bows, ripped open the top, and poured the contents into his palm. Or tried to. His hands were shaking so much the almonds scattered. They bounced off the table, his knees, the hardwood floor . . .

Cruz peered into the bag. It was empty. "Nuts!"

Frustrated as he was, he couldn't help but smile at his pun. Cruz started scooping up almonds. He was dropping them back into the pouch when he spotted a folded slip of aqua paper under the little dish that had held his bread. Sliding it out, he flattened the paper on the tray:

Life is a circle. Sometimes smooth. Sometimes rough. But always a circle.

Another clue!

What could it mean? Might be best to try breaking it down. Take it one sentence at a time.

Life is a circle.

A circle was round. Duh. What else? A circle kept going forever. It had no end. But life *did* end. So, life really wasn't a circle, was it? Unless the clue was referring to what they'd learned in biology about the life cycle of plants and how seeds are distributed by such factors as wind and animal droppings so new plants could grow. Yet, that didn't seem to apply here. Maybe he ought to go on and circle back to it. He grinned. Another pun.

Sometimes smooth. Sometimes rough.

Eggs were smooth. But not really circular. More oval. Apples and grapes and scoops of ice cream were all smooth. Was it saying that food was life? Could be. What about rough circles? He could think of lots of those: basketballs, coconuts, snowballs, tires. But what did any of those have to do with life? Getting to his feet, Cruz began to pace the perimeter of the room as he pondered the clue. Maybe it wanted him to look for a circle that was both smooth and rough? Did such a thing even exist?

Smooth. Rough. It seemed more likely the clue was talking about two distinct circles.

Two circles. He stopped abruptly. In the flickering light of the oil lamps, Cruz frantically dug in his pockets until he found the two washers from his mother's box. He stared at the smooth and ridged metal rings in his palm. Could these be what the clue was referring to?

Only one sentence remained: *But always a circle.*

Always.

It sort of sounded like he was supposed to find another circle to match those he had.

Cruz's eyes went up and down the paneled walls, looking for an indentation or a painting or anything that resembled the washers in his hand. He'd searched the first two walls and was rushing across the room to the opposite wall when he froze mid-step. Cruz dropped his gaze. Sitting at the little table, he hadn't noticed that the floor was inlaid with two different-colored woods—one light and one dark—creating a circular pattern. Beneath his feet was a big circular maze! Cruz rushed to the center of the maze. Dropping to his knees, he ran his hands over the wood, feeling for loose floorboards. He found none. The seams were solid. Cruz sat back. He didn't get it. This was clearly another circle. He had followed the clue precisely.

Or had he?

His mother had told him to walk the path in front of him. "Remember," she had said, "there are no shortcuts to any place worth going."

But he *had* taken a shortcut to get to the middle of the maze. Cruz had cheated.

Dashing to the outside of the circle, Cruz found the marked entrance. He began to walk it, but this time he stayed on the light wood inlaid between two darker, curving lines. Weaving back and forth, Cruz couldn't help thinking that either there were no dead ends in this maze or he was really, really lucky. He was breezing through it. Halfway in, he knew it couldn't be luck. He'd heard of mazes like this. There was a special name for them. What was it? It was on the tip of his tongue.

With each turn, Cruz wound closer and closer to the center of the circle. It was kind of fun. Once he realized he was not going to hit a roadblock and have to backtrack, Cruz could let his feet take over while his mind considered more important things—like whether he would find the cipher or another clue at the end of the labyrinth. Labyrinth!

That was its name. No dead ends. No tricks. No getting lost. As long as you followed the path in front of you, you were sure to reach the center. And here he was! Taking the final turn, Cruz stepped into the center of the labyrinth. He looked down.

Now what?

Cruz felt a slight vibration. The floorboards beneath him were beginning to separate!

22

▶**LIKE THE APERTURE** on a camera lens, the boards were moving apart. Cruz hopped out of the way until the sections stopped. A three-foot space had opened up in the floor. There, tucked into the rocky foundation, was a purple ball slightly smaller than a baseball. The top half of the ball began to slowly open.

Cruz leaned in, tilting so far forward he nearly toppled into the hole. The lower part of the ball contained two round side-by-side holes. One hole had a notched edge, the other didn't. Cruz slipped the ridged washer into the first spot and the smooth washer into the second. He had barely enough time to pull his hand back before the sphere began to close.

Moments later, the purple orb emitted a beam of white light. It wavered, steadied, and Cruz saw...

His mother.

Her head swept right, then left, until she spotted him. Her face held no expression, and he suspected that the holo-program was now trying to identify him.

Cruz stood completely still, his heart thumping in his ears.

Ten seconds passed before her eyes softened. She grinned at him. Blew a quick kiss. And was gone.

The ball closed, flipped over, and the bottom half, which was now the top half, began to open. Cruz crept toward it. The lid came up and there, sitting in the middle of the circle was a pie-shaped slice of black marble.

The sixth cipher!

Cruz reached for the stone before the ball could close again. Clutching it in his fist, he headed for the door. Hurrying back down the passage to the entry hall, he called out, "Hello, hello!"

No one answered or appeared.

Cruz stuffed his feet into his shoes, threw on his coat, and flung on his pack. "Thank you for everything!" Only his own voice echoed back to him, though Cruz had a feeling that he had been heard.

He hurried out of the temple. It took him less than three minutes to fly down the hundreds of steps it had taken him 15 minutes to trudge up last night.

If he could get to the ticket booth in half the time it took him to reach the Tiger's Nest, he would make it back to the hotel before the temple even opened to the public for the day! Prescott, Rook—no one would be able to catch him. Cruz jogged across the bridge past the waterfall and began climbing the 400 steps he'd come down to reach it. This was the hardest leg of the hike. All he had to do was make it to the top of the hill and he would be home free. Huffing, Cruz hopped off the last step and took a sharp right, following the rickety, thin handrail along the cliff's edge.

"Cruz Coronado!"

Cruz froze, his chest heaving. Ten feet ahead, a man blocked the trail.

And that man was Malcolm Rook.

His hair was much shorter and had a weird tangerine tint to it, but Cruz would know the old Academy librarian anywhere. Mr. Rook was holding his arm straight out in front of him. A gun was pointed directly at Cruz. "I don't want to hurt you!" he shouted. "I just want the cipher."

Yeah, right. I've heard that before.

His eyes darting, Cruz saw that his escape options were limited. To his right, a sheer wall of rock stretched to the sky. To his left, beyond the thin handrail, was the deadly drop to the valley below. Cruz spun to go back the way he'd come and got his first look at the temple in daylight. The monastery was much larger than he'd realized. The chain of buildings hugged the mountainside, stair-stepping around a wall of craggy dark slate. The morning dew made the golden roof sparkle. Could he make it back?

"Don't even think about it!" warned Mr. Rook, reading his mind. He slowly turned his hand sideways, closing one eye to line Cruz up in his site. "Ever seen one of these? This baby uses a force field to mask the sound of the shot, meaning you'd be on the ground before you even realized I'd pulled the trigger. Wild, huh? Like something you'd find at Explorer Academy."

"You're wrong," yelled Cruz. "We're explorers. Not killers."

"I told you. I only want the cipher."

Cruz moved his arm, putting his fist behind his back. "I don't have it. I'm in the wrong place."

Mr. Rook cackled. "How dumb do you think I am?"

"I probably shouldn't answer that," muttered Cruz.

"You can give it to me or I can take it," barked Mr. Rook. "So, this is what you're going to do. Take off your backpack. Put it on the ground. Place the cipher and your phone on the ground, too."

Cruz glanced at the handrail, then at the wall. If only he could spin around...

Something whizzed past his nose. Cruz jumped back.

"The next one won't miss!" cried Mr. Rook. "Do what I tell you."

Cruz knew he had no choice. He slid out of his pack and set it down on the path, along with his phone. Opening his fist, he reluctantly let the piece of black marble slide onto the nylon pack. He sure hated to lose this.

"I knew you had it," growled Mr. Rook. "Turn around, hands in the air."

Cruz obeyed. He was facing the rail, staring at the pine forest on the opposite hill. He couldn't believe it. He'd come all this way, figured out

the clue and walked the labyrinth to find the cipher, only to lose it to nasty Mr. Rook!

Out of the corner of his eye, Cruz caught movement to his left. Someone was on the stairs! Cruz turned his head ever so slightly . . .

Taryn?

What was she doing here?

Green eyes widening, she put a finger to her lips. Cruz realized his adviser was hidden by the corner of the cliff. From where he stood, Mr. Rook couldn't see her.

"Go back down the stairs, Cruz," ordered Mr. Rook. "Go all the way to the bridge. I don't want to see you. I don't want to hear you. Stay at the bridge for a half hour. *Move!*"

Cruz began walking. Once he'd made the turn, he was out of Mr. Rook's line of sight. Taryn had flattened herself against the rock. "Go on past me," she directed him as he came down the steps. "Go, go, go!"

"What are you—"

"Run! And keep running."

Cruz tore down the stairs as fast as his shaky legs could go, thoughts and questions ping-ponging in his brain.

Mr. Rook is going to get the cipher. What is Taryn going to do? She isn't going to try to stop him, is she? How did she even know I was here?

Cruz tripped. He latched on to the handrail to keep from going over the hillside. That was close! About 50 steps down, Cruz felt safe enough to glance over his shoulder. He expected to see Taryn hurrying toward him. But that's not what he saw.

At the top of the stairs, Mr. Rook and Taryn were locked in battle! The librarian had clamped his hands on to Taryn's shoulders. She had her fists up and was trying to break his grasp with her forearms. As the two struggled, their thrashing kicked up a dust cloud. Cruz raced back up the stone stairs as fast as he could go. His heart hammered against his ribs. He was on fire from his lungs to his legs.

Hold on, Taryn! I'm on my way!

Cruz had less than a dozen steps to go when he saw the final push.

A coat billowed out, like the mainsail of a boat in a brisk wind. An arm stretched upward, fingers spread wide. And then there was nothing. Not a sound. Not a cry. Nothing.

Mr. Rook was gone. He had fallen into the canyon.

Her back to him, Taryn dropped to her knees. Cruz rushed to her. "Thank goodness! I don't know how you did it, 'cause that guy is twice your—"

Breathing hard, Taryn's eyes did not meet his. She was looking down at her chest. Blood was seeping through her shirt.

Cruz gasped. "You've been shot!"

"Had to . . . stop him." Taryn glanced up. "He was going to shoot you . . . anyway . . ." She slumped forward. Cruz caught her, easing her onto her side.

"Take it easy." Cruz struggled out of his jacket. Crumpling it, he gently placed it under her head. "I'm going to the monastery for help."

She reached out. "Stay."

"But, Taryn, I have to—"

"Ground rules . . . remember?" She coughed. "And I told you . . . not to look back."

She was lecturing him? Now? Cruz had to go. If he didn't, she'd . . . she'd . . .

"Taryn, I'll be back before you know it," said Cruz. "It'll only take me a few minutes . . ."

"Stay," she rasped.

That's when Cruz understood. Even a few minutes would be too many. Suddenly, a deep and terrible ache filled his chest. Cruz had never felt such intense pain. No, that wasn't true. He'd felt it before. Seven years ago. His eyes welling, Cruz knelt beside her.

Taryn pressed the cipher into his palm. "Take care of Hubbard, truth seeker."

She had not called him that since the day Dr. Hightower had expelled him.

"I will . . . of course I will, but I won't need to. You're gonna be fine—"

"He loves you." Emerald green eyes probed his. "So do I."

"Taryn … I'm so sorry about … all of this," he choked. "I … I love you, too."

Long after she was gone, after the sun had risen and the towering pines had spread its beams into soft fans of light, Cruz stayed with her. Taryn had protected him, as she'd promised. Now it was his turn.

As he knelt beside her on the trail, Cruz told his adviser everything he'd kept secret from her. He thanked her for helping him. For guiding him. For believing in him. And then, when there was nothing more to say, Cruz wrapped his hands around hers. He kept them warm for as long as he could.

23

►**CRUZ STARED** blankly at the helicopter blades whirling to a stop. He wondered if anyone had come up to *Orion*'s weather deck to meet them. He hoped not. He didn't know how long he could pretend to be brave.

No one said a word as they waited for Captain Roxas to open the door. Cruz hadn't eaten all day. Hadn't slept in almost 36 hours. Didn't want to.

Aunt Marisol said it was shock. Cruz's dad said it was grief. Cruz knew it was neither. It was guilt. If Cruz hadn't gone to the Tiger's Nest by himself, none of this would have happened. Taryn should have been coming home with them. She should have been giving everyone advice and planning Funday activities and crocheting more clothes for Hubbard.

Weary, Cruz climbed out of the aircraft, took his gear, and began lugging it across the helipad. He felt as if his bones would crumble and blow away. Behind the ship's wake, only a tiny strip of orange remained above the rolling blue horizon. *Orion* was heading into darkness.

Leading the way to the roost, Lani stopped. Dropping her duffel and pack, she whirled to face them. "Before we go inside, I have something to say."

Cruz tensed. He knew what it was and he deserved it. There was no explanation, no excuse, no apology that he could give that would be good enough to justify what had happened. And, of course, nothing could bring Taryn back. Taking a shallow breath, Cruz steeled himself for her anger.

"What happened at the Tiger's Nest"—Lani lifted her voice over the gusts whipping across the weather deck—"it's my fault."

Cruz's jaw fell. "What?"

"It's true." She looked at him, her eyes welling. "If I hadn't told you that I recognized Prescott from the observatory, you wouldn't have felt like you had to go to the monastery by yourself—"

"No, Lani, no." Cruz shook his head. "You had nothing to do with—"

"It's my fault, too," said Emmett. His emoto-glasses were transparent with the faintest hint of pink. "I didn't take Roewyn seriously. I figured she was lying and that her dad sent her to throw you off the trail. I never thought Mr. Rook would show up in Bhutan, not in a million years. Plus, I went to bed early . . . I didn't even hear you leave the room. I should have—"

"Stop!" cried Sailor. "You're both wrong."

Here it came. Cruz knew he could always count on Sailor for the truth, even if he didn't always want to hear it.

"Listen to me." Sailor put her hands on her hips. "The only person who's responsible for what happened to Taryn is Mr. Rook. Nobody else. Mr. Rook has been after Cruz from the beginning. Even when Cruz saved his life, he wasn't grateful. He didn't change. He's still an evil guy. I mean, he *was* an evil guy. Mr. Rook did this. None of you are to blame for what happened to Taryn. Do you hear me? None of you."

Lani wiped her eyes. "O-okay."

Emmett and Cruz nodded, too.

"All right, then," said Sailor in her sternest *that's that* voice. She picked up her pack and duffel and marched across the helipad. Cruz, Emmett, and Lani followed.

As they approached the roost, Cruz saw that Aunt Marisol was standing in the little window. Bryndis was beside her. He was glad they'd come.

Most evenings, the explorers' deck on *Orion* bustled with the students' comings and goings—conversations, laughter, music. Not tonight.

As Cruz, Emmett, Lani, Sailor, and Bryndis padded down the passage, all was quiet.

"Your aunt told you about Taryn, right?" asked Bryndis. "About her getting very sick on her recruiting trip to India?"

"Uh . . . yeah," said Cruz, his heart sinking. "She told us."

Dr. Hightower had come up with the story in order to cover the truth.

"We're all still in shock," said Bryndis.

"Us too," said Lani.

They paused at Taryn's door. A sprig of rosemary tied with white ribbon was leaning against it. There was also a ball of red yarn, a crochet hook, several homemade cards, and a little bowl of popcorn. Cruz bet it was sugar cookie flavored—Taryn's favorite.

"Dr. Hightower said Taryn didn't want a funeral, so we've been leaving things here that remind us of her," explained Bryndis. "The rosemary is from Chef Kristos's herb garden in the greenhouse. Fanchon brought the popcorn. I made a card. You guys want to sign it before I leave it?"

"Sure," said Cruz, his throat tightening.

Everyone took their turn signing the card.

Back in their cabin, Emmett and Cruz quietly unpacked. Cruz slid his mother's box out from under the bed so he could return the items he'd taken with him on the trip. Lifting the aqua lid, he placed the photograph and the key inside. It felt strange not to have the washers, too.

Cruz touched the bag of almonds that looked like the one the monk had given him. It wasn't just similar. It looked identical. The same type of red ribbon tied in a double bow, the same kind of cellophane, and even what appeared to be about same number of nuts in the pack.

Was it coincidence? Or was his mom trying to communicate something?

Curious, Cruz tugged on the end of the ribbon. He pulled the top apart and dumped the nuts into the box. Scattering them with his hand, something shiny caught his eye. Cruz picked up a gold tac pin. It was in the shape of an ankh, the Egyptian symbol for life.

"Emmett, look." Cruz held up the pin. "It was in the packet of almonds my mom left."

His roommate tossed his empty duffel into the closet and came over. "You think it's part of our next clue?"

"I don't know."

"It's almost eight. Are we getting together tonight to open the journal?"

Cruz's hand went to his chest, to the six connected pieces of the cipher hidden under his shirt. "No." Getting to his feet, he tucked the ankh pin into his jacket pocket. "Let's do it tomorrow night. I have something to do before bed."

"I'll bet I know. Does it have something to do with a certain four-legged fuzz ball with a wet nose?"

"Yep."

Emmett knew him well. Turning right out of his cabin, Cruz headed down the explorers' deck, crossing the atrium to the fore faculty and staff passage. He gave two quick knocks on Fanchon's cabin door, then went to his knees. The instant the door opened, a white furry body bounded toward him, ears up and eyes bright. Hubbard leaped into Cruz's outstretched arms. Catching a whiff of bacon and strawberries, Cruz fought the tears that sprang to his eyes. Cradling the Westie

close, Cruz blinked a few times before glancing up at Fanchon. "I promised Taryn I'd look after him."

A crocodile-print head scarf tilted. "I know."

"You do?"

"Mmm-hmmm. Taryn mentioned that Hubbard and you were good
friends."

Cruz kissed the top of the dog's head. "The best."

"I'm glad you came by," said Fanchon. "Come in. I have a favor to ask."

Cruz followed the *splick-splack* of her flip-flops into the cabin. Seeing
an open suitcase on the bed, his breath caught. "Are you leaving?"

"A short visit to Academy headquarters. It's time for my evaluation
with Dr. Hightower. I was hoping you'd take care of Hub while I'm gone."

"Of course." There was nothing that would make him happier!

"It'll only be for four or five days—a week, at most."

Cruz scratched Hubbard between the ears. "I can handle it."

"When I get back we can set up a schedule. I was thinking he could
spend weekdays with me and you could take him on the weekends—if
you're not on a mission, of course. Is that too much for you?"

"It's perfect," he answered. "Plus, I could play with him after school,
too, every day if you wanted..."

"That sounds good, though you might not need to play *every* day."
Fanchon opened a drawer. "Look what I found."

She was holding Planet Pup! After Hubbard had pretty much ignored
the three-in-one robotic dog companion during their testing phase,
Cruz figured Taryn had probably recycled it. "Nice try, Fanchon, but I
don't think he's interested."

Too late. The tech lab chief was already clipping the small remote to
the dog's collar to sync with Hubbard's brain waves. She flipped on the
power switch and gently released it. It hovered in the air, then dropped
to a few inches above the floor.

As before, the dog merely stared at it.

Cruz let out a sigh. "Fanchon, he's probably not going to—"

Click!

The curved stick section of the disk had detached from the side of the bot. It flew across the room, landing on the floor near the veranda door. Hubbard bounded after it, picked it up, and brought it back to Cruz. The dog opened his mouth. The stick fell to within an inch of the floor and then zipped away again, only to drop next to the bed. Hubbard ran to fetch it.

Cruz couldn't believe it. "He knows exactly what to do now!"

"Taryn *did* say she'd work with him," said Fanchon.

"We've got to show Shristine, Weatherly, and Felipe," said Cruz, his breath catching when he spoke Felipe's name. Cruz was beginning to question whether his friend was, in fact, the Nebula spy. If Felipe *was* Jaguar, he hadn't bothered to pass along the information to Nebula that Cruz had fed him about going to Madagascar. Plus, that night in the laundry compartment Emmett had seen Felipe's fancy spy goggles, but he hadn't actually seen Felipe's face. Anybody could have "borrowed" Felipe's night-vision glasses, right? Cruz couldn't shake the feeling that they had yet to uncover the true identity of Jaguar.

Planet Pup zipped past Cruz's elbow. It flew out the open door and made a sharp aft turn with Hubbard in hot pursuit.

Cruz let himself smile.

As usual, Taryn had kept her promise.

AT EIGHT O'CLOCK THE NEXT MORNING, Professor Modi strolled into Manatee classroom. "Good morning, explorers."

"Good morning," they answered.

"I was shocked and saddened to hear about Taryn Secliff, as I'm sure all of you were." Their instructor headed to the front of the room. "Dr. Eikenboom has instructed me to let you know that he will be a leading grief counseling sessions. More information will be coming about that soon. In the meantime, if there's anything I or any of the faculty can do to help you get through this difficult time, please let us know. We are here to help. Taryn will be greatly missed," said Professor Modi. "However, I will not miss how she used to beat me at chess."

Cruz managed a slight grin.

"Before we begin, I have some good news," said Professor Modi. "One of the conservation teams we worked with on Mahé sent a video."

The holo-screen appeared, and the classroom lights went down.

At first, Cruz didn't see anything. He stretched forward. He wasn't the only one. Was there a problem with the video? A low buzz went through the room.

There *was* something there. They could see the camera lens moving. It was pushing up through dirt. No, not dirt. Sand! The camera tipped forward, caught the sunlight, and hundreds of baby sea turtles came into view. They were scurrying away from the camera, scooting down the beach as fast as their tiny flippers could paddle.

"It's the EggsTend!" cried Sailor. "It has babies!"

"It does, indeed," said Professor Modi. "The robotic egg has been monitoring and protecting this nest of green sea turtles on Mahé ever since it was activated. For those of you who were not aware, the EggsTend was a robotics Funday project and the brainchild of Blessica, Kwento, Emmett, and Kat. Great work, team!"

Everyone clapped. Dugan let out his usual earsplitting wolf whistle. Cruz turned to congratulate Emmett but was blinded. Emmett's emoto-glasses were glowing like the sun!

"The sea turtle conservation team says the EggsTend worked so well, they want to deploy several more," added Professor Modi. "I guess we know what Team EggsTend will be doing on their weekends from now on, don't we?"

The explorers snickered.

"I do have one final announcement to make," said Professor Modi. "I've been informed that Professor Gabriel's surgery was more complicated than the doctors expected."

The laughter quickly died away.

"He's fine, he's completely fine," their teacher rushed to say, "but he'll need additional recovery time, along with some physical therapy. In light of that, Professor Gabriel has decided to take the remainder of the semester off. He'll join us again next fall."

Cruz joined in with the chorus of sad moans. Professor Gabriel was one of his favorite teachers. Cruz had hoped— they'd all hoped—that he'd soon return.

"So, you're going to be teaching us for the rest of the year?" asked Dugan.

"Uh ... actually, no. Dr. Hightower has appointed another instructor to take over this course. Your substitute teacher just arrived this morning." He gestured toward the door. "Please welcome someone you all know quite well ..."

Cruz spun.

"... Dr. Archer Luben."

Seeing the tan, muscular man with the stubbled chin standing in the doorway, Cruz couldn't help but grin. It was good to see him again. Professor Luben was wearing black pants and a matching button-down shirt with the sleeves rolled up.

"Thank you for that warm welcome." Dr. Luben sprinted to the front of the room. "All right, explorers, let's get to work. Please take out your tablets. We'll pick up where you left off last week, discussing renewable energy sources..."

Cruz heard Emmett let out a gasp. His roommate was looking down at his tablet and his emoto-glasses were going crazy, changing color and shape so fast Cruz could barely keep up. Pink circles, yellow trapezoids, lime triangles, then back to pink circles.

"What's the matter?" hissed Cruz.

Emmett was staring at his screen. "You're not gonna believe it...I...I...can't believe it..."

Professor Luben was still talking and, luckily for Emmett, strolling the other way. "Who knows what will be powering our cars in the next century? We already use electricity, air, algae, seawater, hydrogen, and biofuels—what's next, explorers?" Professor Luben was an easygoing guy but had little patience for disruptions. If he turned around and saw Emmett...

Cruz nodded to Emmett's kaleidoscope frames. "You'd better take those off."

Ignoring him, Emmett slapped a palm to his head. "It's crazy...It's actually gonna happen. I never, ever thought it would...not in a zillion years, but it did. I mean, it will."

"What will?" Cruz was confused. "Emmett, what's wrong?"

"Not a thing." His roommate whipped off his glasses a second before Professor Luben swung their way. "You're going, Cruz. Dad got you in. You're going to the Archive!"

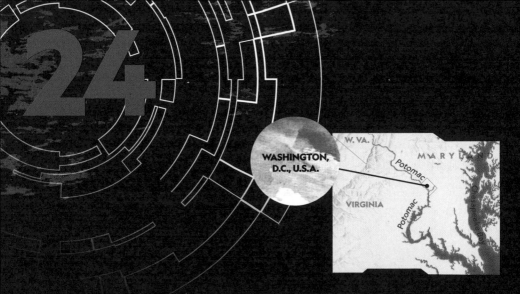

WASHINGTON,
D.C., U.S.A.

W. VA.

MARYLAND

Potomac

VIRGINIA

Potomac

▶**THORNE PRESCOTT** *tapped
the brakes, making sure to keep a safe distance from the silver car
ahead of him. No sense arousing suspicions. Prescott had tailed
Dr. Alec Lu to Reagan National Airport, watched the museum curator pick up Cruz Coronado, then followed the pair as they drove
into downtown Washington, D.C.*

*A few days ago, Zebra had tipped him off that Cruz was headed
to the Academy for a secret meeting. The agent had told him it
had something to do with the Society and that Emmett's dad, a
curator with the Academy's museum, was involved. That was all
the intel Zebra could provide. But it was enough.*

*Cruz had to be going after the seventh piece of the cipher.
What else could it be? If Dr. Lu was in on it, that meant the cipher
had to be hidden somewhere in the Academy's museum. Except
the car containing Dr. Lu and Cruz was turning off 14th Street N.W.
onto Independence Avenue. They were heading east, away from
the Academy. Strange. Maybe the pair was planning another stop
along the way. Prescott made a right at the corner. Both cars were
now traveling toward the U.S. Capitol Building.*

*Prescott's phone was ringing. "Answer," he directed the onboard
computer. "Hello?"*

*"Cobra!" It was Brume. His boss had spoken only one word but
Prescott knew he was furious.*

He deliberately kept his voice calm. "Yes, Lion."

"I don't have much time. Make it short."

"We had Cruz under surveillance from the minute he landed at

Paro," explained Prescott. "Cruz tried to give us the slip. Meerkat followed. I guess he tried to grab the cipher or confront Cruz . . . I'm not sure. Cruz had a bodyguard, who took out Meerkat."

"So, he did your job for you?"

"Uh . . . she." He knew better than to debate the point, but Prescott's job was supposed to be to pretend to work with Rook. Not kill him. At least, not yet.

"I take it you don't have any pieces of the cipher," barked Brume.

"No." Prescott glanced up at the approaching dome of the Capitol. "But we will."

He heard a skeptical grunt.

"I've got him under surveillance as we speak, sir."

Cruz's car was turning again. This time left, onto First Street S.E. behind the Capitol. Prescott followed. In front of him, the car slowed. It was turning into a driveway with a security checkpoint. Stepping out of a guard post, an officer waved them through to a small parking area.

Prescott frowned. What were they doing here?

"Whatever you do, don't let him out of your sight," barked Brume.

"I won't, sir."

The line went dead.

Pulling up to the curb, Prescott watched the silver car park. Cruz got out. So did Dr. Lu. The curator looked like his son, Emmett. Taller, of course, but the thick dark hair, brown eyes, and angular chin were the same. Dr. Lu put an arm around Cruz's shoulders and led him toward the wide concrete steps. Prescott glanced up at the imposing gray building with its grand columns and soaring arches.

Could the cipher really be here? At the Library of Congress?

Prescott found a parking spot a few blocks away, then quickly walked to the building. He did not go inside, deciding to take cover in the shadow of a dark archway where he could keep his eyes on the silver car.

He would wait for the pair to return. Then he would do what Rook couldn't. Prescott would take the cipher from Cruz, destroy it, and put an end to this madness once and for all.

25

"DR. LU? I'm . . . uh . . . a little confused," said Cruz as they headed down the marble stairs to the basement of the Library of Congress. "I thought we were going to—"

"Uh-uh-uh." Leading the way, Emmett's dad turned. He held up a finger. "Not here."

They continued down three more flights of stairs, through a security door, walked a dark hallway that smelled like moss and had to be a couple of football fields long, through another security door to, finally, end at an elevator.

There were no buttons on the wall for up or down. Only a lock. Dr. Lu put a key in the lock and turned it. Immediately, the door slid open. They stepped inside. Cruz saw just one button. The curator pushed it. And down they went. Cruz searched above them for a screen that would indicate how many stories they were dropping. There was none.

"School going well?" asked Emmett's dad.

"Uh . . . yeah."

"That's good." Dr. Lu smiled. "My son's not giving you any trouble, is he?"

Cruz returned the grin. "Nah, he's great. Whoa!" His stomach felt like it had fallen into his shoes. They were dropping faster and faster.

"Hold on," instructed Dr. Lu.

Cruz grabbed the rail. A few minutes later the elevator slowed, then

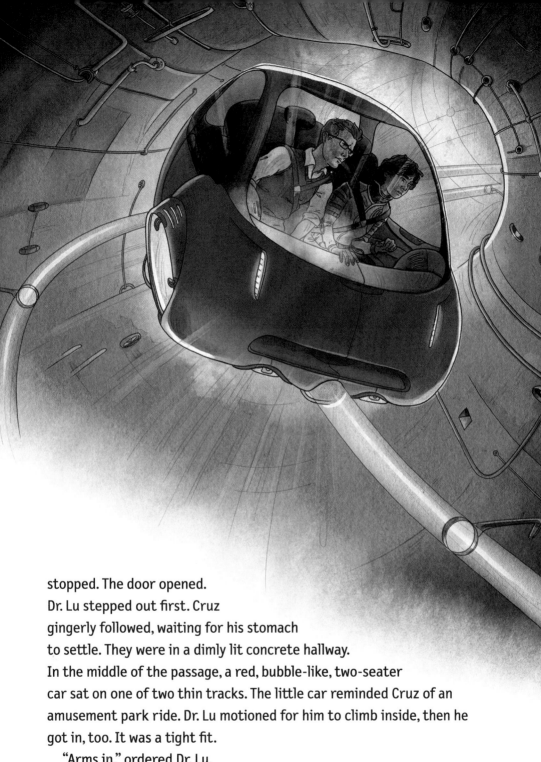

stopped. The door opened.

Dr. Lu stepped out first. Cruz gingerly followed, waiting for his stomach to settle. They were in a dimly lit concrete hallway. In the middle of the passage, a red, bubble-like, two-seater car sat on one of two thin tracks. The little car reminded Cruz of an amusement park ride. Dr. Lu motioned for him to climb inside, then he got in, too. It was a tight fit.

"Arms in," ordered Dr. Lu.

No sooner had Cruz tucked his elbows to his sides than a clear top flipped over his head. It latched on to the front of the vehicle and their little car started rolling down the track. It began to speed along, making several sharp turns. Cruz cleared his throat. "Dr. Lu?"

"I know what you're going to ask." The curator gave him the same cocked eyebrow Emmett used when making a point. "You thought the Archive was beneath the Academy. It is. It's also under much of downtown D.C. It takes a lot of space to store the world's greatest treasures, you know."

That made sense.

"We have several secret entrances to the vault," continued Emmett's dad. "I thought it was safer to take you in this way, in case Nebula had someone watching."

A shiver skipped down Cruz's spine. He wondered how much Emmett had told his dad about Nebula. Most likely, everything.

The bubble car came to a stop at a dead end. They got out and went through yet another security door. This one led to a room. Inside, Cruz saw long rows of benches and lockers. Dr. Lu led him to a rack of white hazmat suits. Cruz recognized the large *A* on the front—these had to be the BUSSs, the Bioluminescent Universal Safety Suits that Emmett had spotted in the holo-image.

"Each of us will need to put one on before we can go in," said Dr. Lu.

Cruz removed his jacket and shoes, stepping into the BUSS Dr. Lu handed him. The sleeves hung well past his fingertips, and he had to scrunch up the legs in order to get into the matching shoes, which were also too big. Cruz put on his gloves, then lowered the clear mask attached to his hood over his face. He heard it self-seal, and a second later felt a cool breeze on his neck. The oxygen had kicked on.

Dr. Lu took one look at Cruz in his oversize suit and laughed. "I guess no one ever expected a kid to go inside the Archive. You'll be the first, Cruz."

Cruz was excited but nervous. "We wear these to protect the artifacts, right?"

"That is their primary function. The carbon dioxide we exhale, the oils on our skin, the bacteria that we carry—all of these things can damage paper, ink, paint, photographs, metals, and other assorted and alien mediums."

Did he say alien?

"The suits also provide a natural individual light source that doesn't require maintenance and allows for ease of communication with the computer and one another," said Dr. Lu. "You'll see how it works once we're in there."

Once they were suited up, Dr. Lu led Cruz out of the locker room. They had to pass through several security checkpoints before arriving at a black, shiny glass wall much like the one Cruz had encountered beneath the minaret. Cruz saw no camera, biometric scanner, or computer screen. He hung back. After what happened at the Taj Mahal, he was not about to touch anything.

"Cruz, what you are about to experience you cannot reveal to anyone," said Dr. Lu. "Do you understand? Not to your family, your teachers, or your friends. Not even to Emmett. I know how close the two of you are. It'll be a hard secret to keep. Are you up for it?"

"I am," swore Cruz. But was he?

"All right, then." He stood tall. "Let's proceed."

A moment later, the wall swished to one side.

"How did it know you?" wondered Cruz.

"Cardio biometrics," answered Dr. Lu. "Just the way that no two fingerprints are alike, no two hearts are identical. Hearts are unique in shape and how they squeeze and swell as they beat. As we stood here, the Doppler system was decoding the geometry and rhythm of your heart and checking it against the database to make a match."

"It was? But I don't work here. How would it—"

"Thanks to your OS band, we've had your cardio signature on file since the day you arrived at the Academy."

"We," of course, meant the Synthesis.

Dr. Lu waved for Cruz to go in.

He took a deep breath. This was it! The moment he'd been waiting for!

Cruz stepped into the Archive. He looked at his hands. They were glowing blue! So was the rest of him!

Gazing out through the clear visor on his hood, Cruz saw a warehouse-size room that reminded him of the CAVE—black walls, black ceiling, black floor. Recessed lights dotted the ceiling. In their illuminated BUSSs, people moved between acrylic glass cases placed several feet apart. Lit from within, there were hundreds of cases. They stretched as far as Cruz could see. The Archive was like an infinite museum. And as quiet. The only sound was the squeak of rubbery soles against a shiny black floor.

Dr. Lu led Cruz through the center of the room, following a dotted blue line on the floor that appeared as he walked. Cruz felt as if he were wearing clown shoes. He had to lift his feet so he didn't trip. They strolled past cases containing beautiful statues, intricately painted vases, and jewelry glittering with gems. None of the cases had signs, the way you'd see in a museum, but Cruz recognized many of the treasures, such as the famous gold mask of King Tutankhamun and Michelangelo's "David" sculpture. A hunk of rock about four feet high and three feet wide caught his eye. It couldn't be! Chiseled writing covered the gray slab from top to bottom, side to side. There were three distinct sections of carved writing on the flat surface, and thanks to Aunt Marisol, Cruz knew all of them: Egyptian hieroglyphics on the top, late Egyptian demotic writing in the middle, and Greek on the bottom. Cruz stood there, gawking.

Dr. Lu was waiting for him, but Cruz had to know. "Is this...?"

"The Rosetta Stone."

"You mean, *the* actual—"

"The rock that holds the key to unlocking the meaning of ancient Egyptian hieroglyphics. It was discovered in Egypt by Napoleon's troops."

"I know, but I thought that—"

"It was in the British Museum?" Emmett's dad grinned. "So do the British."

"Aunt Marisol is never going to believe—"

"You can't tell her, Cruz, remember?"

He winced. "Right."

"Take a look at this." Dr. Lu gestured to a case that held a gold crown covered in rubies and pearls, topped with a cross. "It's the Tudor crown that King Henry the Eighth and his daughter Elizabeth the First wore." He raised an eyebrow. "The history books say it was broken up and the gems sold off in the seventeenth century. Of course, we know the truth." Dr. Lu held up a finger, and Cruz realized someone was talking to the scientist in his headset. After a moment, Dr. Lu said, "Come along, Cruz, we only have so much time."

"There's a time limit?"

"In the Archive? Always."

They hadn't even made it a quarter of the way through the room when the floor dots took them to the left toward the wall. They went through another security door and down a hall, passing a glass partition. On the other side of the glass was an enormous screen—it had to be 30 feet high and twice as long. Photographs of jewels, artifacts, and artwork filled the screen.

"That's the lost treasures room," said Dr. Lu. "We don't just protect rare and important documents, books, and other treasures. We also try to find those that have disappeared or have been stolen."

In the bottom corner, Cruz saw a picture of an oil painting. The subject wasn't anything extraordinary: a big bouquet of yellow poppies in a dull brown vase. A stem of three red poppies was drooping over the side of the vase. Cruz liked the contrast of the red against so much yellow. He couldn't say why. Maybe it was because red was Taryn's favorite color.

"The one in the corner is a van Gogh," said Dr Lu. "It's called 'Poppy Flowers.' Stolen, I'm afraid. Worth more than fifty million dollars."

Cruz whistled between his teeth. "Can a thief sell it for that?"

"On the black market? Maybe. Often, though, word gets out and it's too risky for a thief to sell. He or she must sit on it, hoping they'll be able to smuggle it to an unscrupulous rich buyer somewhere. That's why we'll often locate priceless paintings in attics and basements.

They've been given to heirs or sold off at yard sales to people who have no idea they have a valuable piece of art."

"Do you have 'Starry Night' in the Archive, too?" asked Cruz, thinking of one of Vincent van Gogh's most famous paintings.

"What do you think?"

"I've seen that one at New York's Museum of Modern Art," said Cruz, snickering. "Well, I *thought* I had." He gazed at "Poppy Flowers" one last time. "I hope you find it."

"We will," he said. "Eventually."

The blue floor dots were leading them to another security door at the end of the hall.

"Here's where we're going: the science library," said Dr. Lu.

Inside, the room was filled with row after row of enclosed glass bookshelves. Nothing was exposed to the air. As before, Dr. Lu followed the dots on the floor, which took them on a short journey through the stacks to an unmarked shelf.

"Security protocols say we are not allowed to take any of these books more than five feet away from their assigned shelf," said Dr. Lu. "That's why we had to bring *you* to *it.*"

He tapped a code into the security panel and a lock on the door released. Dr. Lu carefully opened the hinged pane. Cruz spotted the books Emmett had seen on the PANDA video: *De Revolutionibus Orbium Coelestium* by Nicolaus Copernicus, and next to that *On the Origin of Species* by Charles Darwin, *Relativity* by Albert Einstein, and *Dialogue Concerning the Two Chief World Systems* by Galileo. He saw more books, too. *Silent Spring* by Rachel Carson and something with a very long title in Latin about mathematics from Isaac Newton. Seriously? *The* Isaac Newton?

The Archive *was* going to be a hard secret to keep!

Dr. Lu reached for a slim spine and brought it out. It was a basic five-by-seven sage green notebook with no title. Only a name was scrawled near the top in black pen: P. Coronado. It wasn't much to look at, but to Cruz, it was everything.

When Cruz reached for the logbook, Dr. Lu stopped him. "There's something else."

Oh, man! What now?

"I am only allowed to let you see page seventy-two—the one that showed up on the PANDA scan. That's the deal I made to get you in here." The curator held up his index finger. "One page."

Was he serious? What if his mother didn't explain what mistake she made on that page? Or how the formula would change his destiny? This was crazy!

"It's not enough," protested Cruz. "I know I can't take the book with me, but why can't I see more of what she wrote? What harm is there in that?"

"I don't know, Cruz. I don't make the rules." He glanced up at the clock. "We're running out of time. Do you accept the conditions or not?"

"I . . . guess . . . I do," he surrendered.

Dr. Lu opened the notebook, fanning the pages until he found number 72. He held it out and turned his head away. "I'm not going to read it. It's for you alone."

Cruz's eyes raced across the page:

> *My breakthrough in cell regeneration has remarkable potential, but my error has resulted in unintended and irreversible consequences. Unfortunately, my glove rolled down on one occasion in the lab, and when I handled the serum I didn't notice the cut on my wrist. Some of the formula spilled into the wound. It was only a few drops but it was enough to alter my DNA, as well as that of my unborn child. I'm all right, and for now it appears that Cruz is, too. He is a happy, healthy baby, thank goodness. My research indicates the full power of the serum will not kick in until he reaches age 13. At that time, however, it could change his entire life. I am unsure of how to explain all of this to him, but I know I must find a way. How do you begin to tell your son his destiny may be to live forever?*

Cruz read the page again. Was she saying…?

"Cruz?"

He felt his shoulder shake. "Uh-huh?"

"We have to go." Dr. Lu snapped shut the notebook. Turning, he placed it back in its space on the shelf, then closed the glass pane. Cruz heard the lock latch. "We're going to go out a different way than we came in, to be safe," said the curator.

"Uh-huh."

"You look pale." Dr. Lu was studying him. "Is your oxygen level okay?"

"Uh-huh."

The floor dots were now red.

Cruz barely remembered following them out of the science room or passing the lost treasures or even getting out of his BUSS. There were more tunnels and another bubble car ride and an elevator that took them to the surface. They came out through a maintenance shed near the Lincoln Memorial, where another car was waiting to take him to the Academy to spend the night.

Cruz had sworn never to reveal to anyone what he'd seen or learned in the Archive. He could not tell his dad, his aunt, his friends, Dr. Hightower—no one. Not that anyone would ever believe him. Cruz barely believed it himself. Was it true? Was it even possible?

Could he really be…

Immortal?

THE TRUTH BEHIND THE FICTION

Seventy-one percent of planet Earth is covered by ocean, which is why protecting it and the creatures that call it home is important to both the Explorer Academy recruits and real-life scientists and explorers at National Geographic.

Like Cruz, Emmett, Bryndis, Lani, and Sailor, scientists rely on many tools to help them explore the ocean, from scuba-diving equipment to remotely operated vehicles (ROVs) to manned deep-sea submersibles. The more we know, the better we are able to keep it healthy for future generations.

VANESSA BÉZY

With turtle survival being increasingly threatened by tourists, development, poachers, and loss of habitat, GPS and drones are becoming critical to the survival of many species. Emmett's EggsTend may be fictional, but it was inspired by the decoy eggs scientists in Central America are testing as a way to track poachers. Fake eggs are implanted with GPS tracking devices, then placed with real eggs in the nests of sea turtles. When poachers steal the clutch, the decoy egg relays data back to the authorities on smuggling routes.

National Geographic Explorer Vanessa Bézy takes on a different, but equally important type of sea turtle monitoring. She uses drones to capture images of the olive ridley sea turtle *arribada*, or arrival,

in Spain. There, mother sea turtles arrive by the thousands to lay their eggs on the crowded beaches. This natural phenomenon has long been a mystery to scientists. By studying aerial footage, Bézy hopes to understand why these turtles gather en masse to certain beaches, and to unlock the secret of their turtle communication. She thinks the unique egg-laying ritual may have to do with safety in numbers. With turtle survival rates becoming more and more threatened, laying their eggs in the same spot at one time increases the chances of survival.

MICHAEL LOMBARDI

In several books in the Explorer Academy series, we see the recruits hopping into submers- ibles to go for a dive, or donning wet suits to scope out life beneath the waves. An avid surfer, Cruz Coronado would *live* in the ocean if given the opportunity. Well, thanks to National Geographic Explorer Michael Lombardi and his colleague New York University professor Winslow Burleson, he could . . . temporarily. Lombardi and Burleson designed the Ocean Space Habitat, a breathable environment that allows divers to sleep with the fishes—literally. The OSH is a portable life-support tent that can be anchored to the seafloor. Divers can go inside the dry, inflatable tent to eat, talk, nap, and decompress. The OSH means humans will be able to go deeper and stay underwater longer than they could using conventional scuba-diving gear. "Think about a naturalist who studies creatures in the woods," says Lombardi. "How much they can observe, document, and learn in an hour-long hike, versus camping out immersed in the environment for an overnight—or two or three. OSH offers this sort of immersive experience rather than simply being a temporary visitor while scuba diving."

SALOME URSULA BUGLASS

Over 90 percent of the world's oceans represent deep-sea habitat, but because it's difficult for humans to access and study these remote underwater dark spaces, most of the life-forms that live there remain a mystery. Beneath layers and layers of water, extreme pressure would crush most nonadapted beings, and it's very dangerous for humans to dive in deeper waters. That's where robots, or remotely operated vehicles (ROVs), play a critical role in overcoming the challenges of exploring life in deeper waters. National Geographic grantee Salome Buglass knows this firsthand. In the volcanic archipelago of the Galápagos, she explores and studies ecosystems on seamounts that are often located in the twilight zone, where some light is still present, or much deeper down—more than 6,000 feet (1,829 m)—where it's pitch black and very cold. Seamounts are underwater volcanoes; they and are known to host a variety of marine life, from algae and sponge gardens to cold-water coral reefs. Using an ROV, Buglass and her collaborators have been able to explore and survey these deep habitats, collecting videos, photos, and samples that have led to the discovery of more than 20 species that are potentially new to science. One of her most exciting discoveries is a deepwater tropical kelp forest on the summit of a seamount. She is currently investigating this habitat in greater detail, as these underwater forests are an important food source and living space for many marine species. Buglass hopes that this new knowledge can support efforts to protect these unknown yet important habitats and can motivate others to further explore deep waters. Our oceans are continuously being altered by climate change, overfishing, and pollution, and we cannot protect, admire, or benefit from ecosystems that we don't even know exist.

DR. EMMA CAMP

In this novel, the explorers learned that overfishing, pollution, and climate change are putting coral reefs in jeopardy around the world. Coral reefs sustain a quarter of all marine life, yet scientists say that since 1970 Earth has lost half of its coral reefs due to coral bleaching. National Geographic Explorer and marine biochemist Dr. Emma Camp has studied coral reefs extensively and has witnessed the effects of the damage firsthand. "Coral is an animal, and it has microalgae that live inside the tissue, and they rely on each other to survive. But under stress, the algae leave the coral, and that's a problem because the coral needs them for food. And that's when the coral becomes bleached."

Scientists fear that at this rate we could lose 90 percent of the world's coral by 2050. But they are coming up with ways to try to give reefs a fighting chance to survive climate change. As the explorers learn in the book, aquaculture, or coral farming, is showing promise as a way to restore damaged reefs on a local scale and boost their resilience to rapid environmental changes.

Corals are cultivated in underwater nurseries, then transplanted where they are needed. Some corals, like brain or great star corals, grow too slowly to be tended in ocean farms. For these, researchers are developing new methods that would allow them to grow corals at a much faster rate inside a laboratory.

Dr. Camp takes another approach: She aims to find and grow corals that are naturally resistant to climate change. "For example, one area that I study is mangrove lagoons. They're shallow, which means the water is warmer, and because of the biological activity, it's more acidic, the oxygen is low, and there is more sediment. In other words, it's a harsher environment. By studying this environment, we can understand how these heartier corals survive, and use that knowledge to better understand coral systems."

EXPLORER ACADEMY

BOOK 6:
THE DRAGON'S BLOOD

34.3841° N | 109.2785° E

"**F**anchon to Cruz Coronado." The tech lab chief's voice crackled through his comm pin. She sounded far away.

"Cruz, here."

"Please report to the tech lab right away."

"Uh . . . sure. Is Emmett with you? Is everything all right?"

No answer.

"Let's go, Hub," said Cruz, attaching the dog's leash. "We'll get your walk in . . . or maybe your run."

They jogged most of the way to the lab. Inside, Cruz and Hubbard waited for the tech lab chief or her assistant to appear from the labyrinth of cubicles, as usual. They hung out for several minutes, but nobody showed up. Weird.

"Fanchon? Dr. Vanderwick?" Cruz glanced down at Hubbard. "I guess she must have gotten busy."

The dog lifted an ear.

Cruz wasn't sure what to do. Should he go or wait a little longer? Fanchon had sounded pretty serious. He didn't want to leave yet. He pressed his comm pin. "Cruz to—"

"Help."

The feeble cry had come from somewhere in the lab.

Overhead, the green lights flickered. Half of them went out.

"Fanchon?" called Cruz.

Silence.

"Come on, Hub." Cruz wrapped the end of Hubbard's leash around his wrist and hurried into the cubicles with the Westie at his side. Which way should he go? He jogged left then right, his eyes searching for a colorful head scarf and apron and pink shoes. He dashed through the lab, poking his head into every work space as he called her name. "Fanchon?"

Cruz came to a stop. They were through the maze. He'd reached the end of the compartment. Fanchon wasn't here. The lights above the cabinets next to him dimmed, then shut off. What was going on? A power surge? A blown circuit?

"*Ruff!*" It was short and sharp—Hubbard's warning bark. The dog retreated a couple steps back into the aisle between the cubicles.

"I know what you mean, Hub," whispered Cruz. "I don't like it either."

Cruz felt something cold snake around his neck.

"Don't move," a digitized voice said into his left ear as icy fingers clamped on to him, "or it'll be the last thing you *both* do."

**Read a longer excerpt from *The Dragon's Blood*
at exploreracademy.com.**

215

ACKNOWLEDGMENTS

Writing is never a solo effort. A writer may light a spark but you can't build a fire without help from others. I am blessed to have so many remarkable people in my life who not only fan the flames, but who also warm my heart. I wouldn't be where I am today without the guidance, passion, and wit of my delightful agent, Rosemary Stimola. She is, simply, the best. I would also be lost without my stellar editing team of Becky Baines, who can keep me laughing through the storm (while she is simultaneously calming it), and Jennifer Rees, who makes me a better writer and does it with a grace, joy, and kindness that few possess. Thank you to my National Geographic family: Jennifer Emmett, Eva Absher-Schantz, Scott Plumbe, Lisa Bosley, Gareth Moore, Ruth Chamblee, Caitlin Holbrook, Ann Day, Holly Saunders, Kelly Forsythe, Bill O'Donnell, Laurie Hembree, Emily Everhart, and Marfé Delano. A special thanks to Karen Wadsworth and Tracey Mason Daniels of Media Masters, who so brilliantly organize my book tours and can make the craziest day fun (even one that includes a car breakdown in the middle of school visits!). Thanks to all the National Geographic explorers who took the time to chat with me about their work. I am deeply grateful to those who also ventured out with me to meet young readers: Zoltan Takacs, Nizar Ibrahim, Gemina Garland-Lewis, and Erika Bergman. Each of you live your convictions and challenge me, and all you meet, to be our best selves. I am indebted to all the booksellers, schools, and libraries across the country that invited me to share the world of Explorer Academy with readers—too many to mention here but you have my heartfelt appreciation for all that you do to inspire kids to read and write. Thank you to every young reader who has ever written to me. I keep all of your letters (so if you haven't yet written to me—do!). Thanks to my parents and family for their faithful support, especially Austin, Trina, Bailey, Carter, and my goddaughter, Marie. I love you beyond words. Finally, thanks to the most selfless person I have ever known, my husband, Bill, who tells me I can do anything and truly believes it.